restless
ness

restless ness

A NOVEL

ARITHA VAN HERK

Red Deer College Press

Red Deer College Press
56 Avenue & 32 Street Box 5005
Red Deer Alberta Canada T4N 5H5

Edited for the Press by Nicole Markotić
Cover and text design by Val Speidel
Cover photograph copyright © 1998 Gary Isaacs/Photonica
Printed and bound in Canada by Webcom for Red Deer College Press

This is a work of fiction. Any resemblance to actual persons, living or dead, is
coincidental. The Palliser Hotel is real, but events in this novel are purely fictional.

Financial support provided by the Alberta Foundation for the Arts, a beneficiary of the
Lottery Fund of the Government of Alberta, and by the Canada Council, the
Department of Canadian Heritage and Red Deer College.

CANADIAN CATALOGUING IN PUBLICATION DATA

Van Herk, Aritha, 1954–
    Restlessness

    ISBN 0-88995-185-3

    I. Title
PS8593.A545R47 1998   C813'.54   C98-910472-9
PR9199.3.V359R47   1998

for Isabel Carrera Suarez,

no molesten!

When I am dead, my dearest,
    Sing no sad songs for me;

> "Song"
> CHRISTINA ROSSETTI

wish you were here

> "Against Travel," in *Dog Sleeps*
> MONTY REID

"Death is a Happy Ending: A dialogue in thirteen parts"

> *Figures in a Ground*
> ROBERT KROETSCH AND DIANE BESSAI

I AM ALONE in a room with the man who has agreed to kill me.

Such an ordinary room, without a hint of gothic fore-boding or sinister intent, the walls papered with some elegant stripe, the curtains hanging a polite two inches above the floor, which is decorously warmed with good quality Berber. Two armchairs hold wide their elbows in front of the window, a bed, substantial and bolstered and duvetted, metaphor for comfort and the sleep that is supposed to knit up raveled sleeves, rafts the center of the room.

I have always wondered at such knitting images because I never could knit, could not hold the yarn so as to give the stitches tension. No matter how Tante Katje offered demon-strations, no matter how she poked the needles under my arms and wrapped the wool around my stiffened fingers.

A white bathroom gleams around the corner, the towels large if not particularly thick, the bathtub deep if a bit scratched. And against the closet door is a metal fold-out suitcase stand, on which the bellhop has perched my bag.

Around the world, people choose to die in the anonymity of hotel rooms. Rented rooms are more considerate than one's own bed or one's own car, the likelihood that loved ones will have to contend with a repercussive mess, the inevitable inquiry, possibly a stinking and forgotten body, every decora-tion of suicide and its grotesque acknowledgments.

I have found the room where I will die, after years spent looking for this particular moment, after years of testing rooms in other countries, other languages, other hotels. And I can now allow myself surprise that the perfect room, with its oddly sweet smell of carpet cleaner and its valanced windows, is here, exactly where I started.

My assassin is less accidental.

I AM NOT a character in a cheap thriller where a detective will break down the door with a bold shoulder, where my body will assume an exotic and silent place at the center of a mystery eventually solved by a slick loner with a penchant for cigarettes and superlative powers of deduction. Elementary, my dear sidekick.

No. I am engaged in an act of hunger, a ravenous plan of escape that I have been working toward for more than a decade. I'm impatient now, more impatient than before, when I pretended to be ready. In Vienna, in the back of a viciously swerving cab. In Jamaica, when I first tasted the sting of ginger beer in the back of my throat. In Brussels, where I finally figured out how.

But always I have waited, listened for the deep gong of a moment's well-tempered agreement, and hesitated. Like Prufrock. Do I dare to eat a peach? Shall I wear the bottoms of my trousers rolled?

Except that I am not afraid.

LEST ANYONE IMAGINE that my impending death is less interesting than how I arrived here, I feel the need to reiterate my happy if substanceless life. Sitting on the edge of this bed, my legs dangling a few inches from the floor (I am not a tall woman), I think of my journeys and their circular arrivals, anticipate my epitaph, how I will lie with the bedcovers resting lightly across my breasts, a barely touched glass of water on the night table, this tumult at last erased.

My chosen assassin tells me I can change my mind right up until he commits the act and finishes my briefly executed life for me. I would, however, now that I have gone this far, have to pay him a kill fee, whether I decide to proceed or not. So we sit uncomfortably on the edge of the bed and pretend to have a conversation while we wait. He waits for me to nod toward him as a signal to proceed, and I wait for him to ask the kind and gentle questions that will lead us toward night.

His hands, I think, are tender, his thumbs oddly double-jointed, one nail trimmed with the blue of hammer bruise. I must imagine his hands because he is, understandably enough, wearing gloves, not black and sinister, but thin-skinned suede gloves that might befit a race car driver sensitive to the wheel.

I think, oddly, that were I in an airplane about to crash, I would want him next to me, and the impending crash would give me an excuse to hold the comfort of his hand. But that is part of his profession. He is required to be comforting, for his are the last arms those who choose dying know.

I WAIT FOR a city to seduce me, to sidle up in a bar and suggest assignation. This happy connection occurs only sporadically. Amsterdam succeeds every time, easily, as if it recognizes my blood connection, my accent tilted but manageable, my vocabulary old-fashioned but adequate. London refuses, as do Trieste and Sydney. They look me over with their jaded barman's eyes and turn away. I am middle-aged, and such urbane sites prefer young woman, thin-boned and louder, with an elbow's cigarette flick, than I have come to be.

But Cairo took to me immediately, without a word, simply pushing me up against a wall and holding me, rough but attentive to my pleasure, my nose alive with cloves and smoke.

And Sarajevo, oh god, Sarajevo with its dry river and anxious gardens—there I could barely stand for the water in my legs, for the taint of muscle pressed against my groin. If only I had been able to manage a language, I could have arranged a good-bye there, my feet planted within the cement outline of Princip's end-of-empire footsteps. Cast in the side-walk. But so much of Sarajevo is rubbled now, beyond the call to prayers in the mosque-soaked morning air I breathed there.

They say you remember a city by its pleasures, what you eat and drink, who your companions are. I remember cities by how far I walk, how much of them I manage to cross on foot, the weariness of my thighs and calves. And I remember cities for the assassins I encounter, their eagerness to kill under-mined by their clumsiness.

James Joyce claimed that Trieste ate his liver; I could claim that Tübingen ate my heart. Now, Tübingen is faint with erasure. All I remember is the maid sitting outside the door with her feet neatly planted beside each other, waiting for us to finish fighting, to vacate the room. When I came out to use the shower, my feet bare, a fragment of towel around me, she raised her head, but quickly, then lowered her eyes. As if ashamed to acknowledge that she had heard my crying.

I CAME TO crave assignations in public parks, declarations of temporary love on benches graceful with wrought iron beside well-trodden paths. Those brief and barely consummated meetings kept me alive for a while. Before my dear one found me, took me in his arms.

And now, now, it is in a hotel room that I will close and fold my limbs.

I turn toward my assassin, who is perched on the edge of the bed as intently as I am.

"Will you take a more comfortable seat?"

"Thanks," he says, and gets up, moves around the bed toward the armchair next to the window. He sinks back, stifles a sigh. He must not betray impatience or surprise; he is required to do what I request.

I study him curiously, his somewhat worn face, the sadness around his eyes. "Wouldn't you rather do this in a park? A hotel room seems so enclosed. Or perhaps a more isolated place, more appropriate, like a graveyard?" I am almost serious.

He nods, accepting my dissatisfaction with the room's chintzy comfort. "It's too risky. Someone would see us."

I can't have that. Can't take the chance of someone stopping my savior midkill.

WE HAVE SIGNED in as if we are a couple, possibly lovers, both of us under assumed names, although of course, I will leave my real, bright-as-a-copper-penny Canadian passport on the night table next to the bed so that I can be easily identified. I prefer my passport photo to the one on my driver's license. And I will need to be identified. After.

The maid will find me in the morning. I feel sorry for that delegation—she will have a shock, a woman dead under the covers. But since I am a stranger to her, perhaps she can bundle me up with the endless sheets that she changes every day, the bathroom floors she scrubs, the towels that she counts and hangs. She will call down, angrily shrill, for her supervisor, who will thunder up the stairs or astride the service elevator and try to slap me awake before calling the house manager, who will call the police, who will call my number and, getting no answer, will call everyone else, including my Tante Katje.

She'll look into my telephone list and call my dear one.

If I were in a foreign country, the Canadian consul would arrange to ship me home, have some kind of coffin loaded into the belly of an airplane. Unless, of course, Katje decreed that I might as well be cremated there, scattered to a foreign wind and thus more easily relegated to my sudden good-bye.

But I am safe in Canada. My own country. Less trouble for everyone, and the insurance ought to be enough for a decent box and a few flowers.

Funny, I assume that I'll be in bed. Perhaps he'll tip me into the bathtub or fold me up in the closet. I look at my assassin, his head resting against the shoulder of the chair, quiet as an accomplice. His gloved hands on the armrests seem separate from him, removed, and I try to see where the

sleeves stop and the leather begins. In Dutch, gloves are called
handschoenen, shoes for the hands, a tougher and more accurate word.

He smiles, shrugs as if to reassure me.

Embarrassed at my stare, I avert my eyes.

⟋◯

"THEY WILL WONDER what to do with my books."

"Does that worry you?"

"I've collected too many, they pile up everywhere because I
don't have enough shelves. They even get trapped between the
covers of my bed."

"The best of lovers."

"Lovers?"

"Books."

"Perhaps my aunt will divide them among my friends."

"Would you like to leave that instruction? It might help you
to relax, knowing that your possessions have a home."

"Leaving instructions seems too deliberate."

"An admission?"

"As if I wanted to tell them how to remember me."

"And don't you want to be remembered?"

I have to think for a moment. His questions lack the
unctuous tones of a counselor or a priest, and his responses
are soft, as if he had trained for the job of comforting the
incipient dead.

"I would rather—be erased."

"Oh," he says sadly. "You will. You will be."

His sadness makes this prospect harder. I wish he were
aggressive, brutally cheerful about his task. But he looks down

at his concealed hands, then lifts his head to catch my eye with a quizzical tilt of his head.

Of course, I don't mean that. I don't want a vicious killer.

He is exactly right for the job. Slow, considerate, letting me take these steps at my own pace, letting me make small talk as I feel my way toward my planned and chosen oblivion.

I HAVE A book with me, a thin strange book by Alberta writer Monty Reid. I don't know how I came to buy it, probably the cover of a woman asleep, holding a pillow, the paws of a black dog next to her.

I've read just enough of *Dog Sleeps* to know its departure, how it calls travel an uninhibited restlessness, a terrible convulsion of some subject searching for a way to inhabit a moment, to declare having been at some somewhere. This could be my hymnal.

Places become both famous and common, their naming rolls off the tongue—*London, New York, Paris*—making us accomplices, assistants to their renown, their bridges and museums, their *air du plein*, their intricate European fame, their sobriquet needing no identification.

I like *Dog Sleeps*. It suits me, quizzical intelligence in a book to read before dying.

I READ GREEDILY, without much discretion, so long as there are words aligned on pages, narrative with language quirks frequent enough to make me pay attention. No romances, no mysteries. Novels mostly, since short story collections exacerbate my restlessness. One story ends and another begins, that story ends and another begins.

There's nothing else to do on airplanes, buses, trains. The movies they show are junk. And other people's private dramas are easier to observe over the edge of a book.

For the last twenty years I feel as if I have been waiting for my life to happen between the pages of a book, the book I am reading while I wait to arrive at the destination I am destined for.

I used to read more before my dear one found me. Now we fall asleep together on the crumpled pages of abandoned novels.

THIS READING HABIT has its effect.

I slum most happily with literary cities. Trieste, Vienna, London, Berlin, Paris. I long to visit Bombay, shrill with Rushdie. Such eloquently documented streets offer excuses for loitering, their libraries replete with achievement, their streets and cafés suggesting a momentum that I have missed and that now I have no choice but to resist, without regret.

THE FIRST TRAVELERS were conquerors, not interested in looking, but in having.

Possession tourists, not so different from today's journeying acquisitors, cameras framing ancient buildings and automatic flashes wearing away fragile surfaces, so that retention becomes destruction.

I've spent my life as a working tourist, expected by occupation to travel, expected to shift between borders and currencies as effortlessly as the birds that fly above. It's my job to travel, and I'm required to travel well.

I TRAVEL TO escape the rotund, belligerent light of the foothills, the knife of high cerulean blue. Light is seldom muted in Calgary, sometimes gray if snow or rain plunges over the city, but that temporary reprieve seems aberrant, and until the dazzle returns, people look puzzled.

Visitors arrive in order to shade their eyes at the teeth miraging the western skyline. Fall and spring are best, for then the mountains are sharp echoes outlined with snow.

And the wind is restless with light. In the world's famous bag of winds, bora and sirocco, harmattan and horse, the chinook alone is omitted, as if it blows too regionally, impossible to name in a sophisticated international context. Only those of us who stem from southern Alberta understand the chinook's playful torment. Everywhere auspicious, the wind in Calgary is consigned to bluster, quick to ascend,

knocking against houses as if to demand admittance, tearing
at the long grasses bending close to the tightly pocked ground.
No argument for romance from its breath, slow to die.

My dear one made me want that wind, want to play in it,
loose my hair to its tangles. Before he came, the chinook
threw grit into my eyes, refused to enfold me in its arms.

EVERY CITY WHERE I've touched down hoards my remains,
the lovers I abandoned sleeping in doorways, the books I have
not read waiting to spring to attention in the windows of
renowned bookshops, the assassins I've evaded hunting other
prey.

My third cousins twice removed are chambermaids in the
hotels where I occasionally stop; my old clothes look much
better strolling the corners of squares and *grachten* than they
do the straight-canyoned streets of Calgary.

I cannot escape myself.

I have tried, tried and tried. And trying, I discovered I was
infected with a terrible suspicion of myself and my inability to
stay still, my dreadful insomnia of place.

AND SO.

I am alone in a room with the man who has agreed to kill
me.

I WANTED THIS transportation to take place in the old
Grand Hotel in Trieste, notorious for the murder of Johann
Winckelmann, Prefect of Antiquities in Rome, whose angel
of death provided him with a quick and merciful end in 1768.
Mourned by Goethe and Cavaceppi, his death an eighteenth
century news item, he had, nevertheless, strolled the Triestine
seafront with his friendly killer for some eight days. My theory
is that the medals stolen from him were an after-the-fact
excuse. Winckelmann arranged his own death. He wanted to
die in Trieste.

In European cities, everyone important has been dead for
years. The cemeteries haunt the living with the sheer weight
of their headstones. Visitors call on the dead, and the living
are the dead's footmen.

The Grand Hotel was long ago razed to make way for less
historical structures. And I have no gold and silver medals to
tempt an assassin.

I have had to resort to hiring someone, someone who, for a
modest fee, will commit a modest act in a modest city.

DUINO WAS ONLY thirteen miles up the coast from Trieste,
and the assassin I was with wanted to go there. But I wanted
to avoid the Byronic excess of that castle, with Rilke's conjunction of anguish.

Trieste is a restless city, Celtic, Roman, Slavic, Frankish,
Austrian, Napoleonic, Austrian, Italian, German, Yugoslavian

18

and now again Italian, with the Vespas buzzing along the waterfront and the food tasting of desire and the turgid Mediterranean, moribund now, locked in its own sadness and the inescapable escapes of a retreating future. Trieste felt like my city, slippery of foot, doomed to a many-colored coat.

DOG SLEEPS WAVES good-bye to "the long hiss of departure after departure," as if travel were distilled by a moment of leaving, when the feet abandon solid ground and step into a train, walk the ramp onto an airplane. Books can do that, pace out the arrangements, tickets, timing, hotel reservations, packing, driving to the airport, taxi to the train station, every step toward the jigsaw of arrival.

Departures begin daily. Taking leave of the very cotton sheets that cover the side of the mattress I sleep on, the floor beside the bed worn by repeated contact with my feet. My arms practice good-bye with their habits, polishing my glass tabletop, pulling thistles from my rock garden, unloading the dishwasher, folding the newspaper exactly in half, grinding the coffee extra fine. Leaving a note for my dear one.

I have taken solace in minutia.

I HAVE DETERMINED to revise my future here, in this logical hotel room, with its excellent amenities, its distinctive plan comfortingly predictable as all hotel rooms are.

Some imperial accident will sweep me away. Like those tourists at Long Beach on the west coast, so mesmerized by the swell and pound of waves that they couldn't fathom the one anomalous crest that rose and rose and crashed around their feet, sucking them down to the rocks below, the water curling them into its embrace. So the Pacific Rim holds another spent shape, delicious in its human warmth, a drowning consummation.

That would have been one way to initiate my revised future: unpredictable waves, placid and forgiving once the act is done. But drowning is an act that I have already suffered, not an experience I want to repeat.

⌒⌒

ONE ASSASSIN HELD my head back under the shower, the water coursing over my nose and mouth so that I could not breathe, could only struggle with his brute imposition. He wanted to frighten me, but he only hurt me. Incompetent, he was.

I drowned as a child, my foot stepping into a deep hole in Buffalo Lake, the sudden engulfment a choking cloak. I drowned and drowned and drowned while around me the shouts of my schoolmates were full of glee at their dunking games. Only casually did a girl pull me erect, stand me upright in the treacherous water. She had no idea I was drowning. I had managed to drown secretly, without the terrible cusp of rescue, its required acknowledgment. I stood in that cold lake water and shuddered with the force of my dreadful escape.

Perhaps then began my interminable journey. I became

adept at pretending that nothing had happened, that I had not been caught in the arms of a persistent and relentless death. Denial became my mantra.

Although my dear one tries to break my silence into pieces, tries to make my thighs whisper, my palms shout, I still pretend that nothing has happened, that I am not shattered, grieving for breath in lungs filled with water. I keep silent the fragility of my body in the face of ruthless interruption.

There are assassins everywhere.

IF YOU TRAVEL enough, you eventually lose the clauses of well-constructed sentences. The framing of questions in languages that are not yours takes on the color of fragment, always fragment, broken thought.

Once in Amsterdam, I needed a safety pin. Just one safety pin to hold up a hem I was too lazy to sew. The hotel where I was staying did not have a safety pin. The newspaper kiosk at the end of the street did not have a safety pin. They sent me to a larger market full of imported French wine and German cookies (in the Netherlands!), but no, no safety pins. I walked from shop to shop, asking for safety pins, which was doubly difficult because my Dutch is passable, but I had forgotten the precise word for *veiligheidspelden*.

So I composed perfectly grammatical questions in one of the most difficult languages on earth but without being able to come up with the object of the question. "Do you have—? *Heeft u? Heeft u?*" But the safety pins that followed, the word symbol for a small metal object used and overused in our tenuous lives (so often I see them in the gym's locker room, the bright hook of metal on the strap of a bra) had vanished. Until, in a fabric shop selling ornate brocades, a bright-faced woman who could have stepped out of a Frans Hals painting laughed and said the word, which I remembered instantly. *Veiligheidspelden*, I whispered to myself as I retraced the street, now able to drop my carefully grammatical request and say only these two words, followed with a question mark. "*Veiligheidspelden? Veiligheidspelden? Veiligheidspelden?*" Finally I found them, in a music store, a card of them hanging on a pillar, the owner charging me not much more than a *dubbeltje*, the diminutive dime that creeps into the seams of Dutch pockets.

I had been reduced to a question mark. So does every sonorous construction flake away, the mouth finally holding only the stone of a noun, a precisely configured noun.

I never dared to tell Aunt Katje. She still lectures me about forgetting my mother tongue, although she should talk. She hasn't been back to Holland since she arrived, and none of her friends speak Dutch.

⌒

IF YOU COME from Calgary, Alberta, a raw city, abstract and premeditated, you cannot help but see the world's terrible dimension. No other eyes have quite the same vision as eyes that have grown up squinting against the light of the foothills, the blue and adamant Rockies cutting the horizon. My sight has slowly faded from that unsubsiding brilliance; light is as capable of eroding time as hands rubbing a stone ledge, year after year.

Unfortunately no vineyards cling to the slopes of the foothills.

THIS AFTERNOON, AN incoming chinook overtakes the arctic wind, cold air colliding against warm and forming a mysteriously colored fog swimming with transparency.

Under the ribbon of mist rising along the river, the sky seems to roar, collect the sound of a lost miracle. Moisture itself is a stranger to Calgary, the city holding its dusty breath through static-ridden winters, briefly reprieved when the snow-eater hovers over the mountains, promising faux summer.

All day the sky shoulders a great arch, softening the mountains. Heavy, looming, it resembles a heavenwide roll of cotton batting, the edge torn in a few places but remarkably distinct in its curve. The sun slides below that bolster and now, late in the afternoon, begins to streak the west an impossible pink.

That's the strangeness of the chinook, its peculiar edge, benign air trapped beneath a glowering face.

I STEP OUT of the cab and up the curb, say my ritual hello to the twin doormen in their archaic uniforms, replicas of 1914, when the hotel opened. They lounge street-wise but attentive under the metal canopy, the cut wrought iron sign swinging just slightly beneath. They are there to whistle me a taxi, call down a delivery truck or even a companion, anything I ask.

The wind kicks up street dust, an empty chips packet swirls by in the gutter, but the afternoon is slower than January, the day a few inches longer, the sun still slanting the sky.

The chinook arch hangs in the west, waiting for a train to

steam toward it, for the river ice to fissure, crack just a little, ease a small sigh of relief.

JANUARY PLANS FOR death, the old and infirm subsiding into stillness because after Christmas there is nothing to look forward to and spring is interminably far away, a word without sensation, the bleak streets slick with ice under hammered metal skies.

But February's longer afternoons quicken pace, reverse October, those evenings just before Halloween pulsing downhill, the trees gaunt and rustling in anticipation of snow.

It is February that I have chosen, February when I want to finish my spate of restless breathing and settle toward earth.

THE CLERK AT the registration desk seems almost sleepy, pushes a form toward me as if I were a stranger here.

I feel utterly exposed, standing here with the bellhop having taken my nicest satchel, an oxblood leather garment case embossed with my initials over its brass lock and buckles, elegant, so elegant I have hardly used it, only dared when I knew I was flying business class. Seldom enough over the years. But useful now, respectable, no other word.

"I'm joining Derrick Atman."

What names do assassins give themselves? It seems a banal name, impossibly plausible.

"I believe that he has already checked in," I add.

"Just a moment." Her fingers hesitate over the computer keys. "Can you spell that for me? One *t* or two?"

I wonder how he arranges his identification—and how does he book a room? Does he have a new credit card issued for every job, and can't the police or the bank track the card back to him? But that isn't my problem here. He's the one responsible for taking care of the details.

The clerk's face remembers wind and horses' manes in that conundrum of a Blackfoot host checking well-heeled guests into a hotel that perches on her inheritance, but she is unsuspicious, which leaves me oddly light-headed. One doubting question from her and I'll burst into tears, confess everything, find myself bundled off to Foothills psychiatric ward, and he—my carefully arranged correspondent—will be left waiting upstairs, pacing the room, flipping through the cable channels. No doubt he's prepared for every possibility, every permutation, clients backing out, changing their minds, even getting lost or having an accidental accident on the way to their arranged accidents. No doubt he's using fake identification, a different name, a disguise.

Standing here at the desk while the clerk hunts for his name, my body wants to waltz across the marble floor below the high ceilings picked out in gilt, so sumptuously tasteful. I grasp my left wrist with my right, hold my feet still with a conscious effort.

Is it the hotel, the clichéd elegance of the foyer, the pulsing chandelier that enhances the lobby's cozy dusk? Or the finality of my entering this final building, pushing through the revolving door as if I too were on my way to a quick Scotch in the bar before driving into the wind, heading to the suburbs for bean stew in the kitchen nook with the family?

"Atman," she says. "Room 531."

She's not supposed to say this, not supposed to tell any occasional inquirer the room number of a guest, but he must have left a note that I'm expected. She hits a sharp clear bell, and the bellhop strides toward me with my leather garment bag, his uniform slightly too large, so that he manages to look shabby despite the spit and polish of his braid and edging. But comforting too, as if he falls asleep in his clothes.

"Five thirty-one," she says, handing him the key, and he follows me across the lobby, the bag over his shoulder, toward the brass-doored elevator bank, where the ghost of Robert Barr, killed when he peered headfirst into the shaft, looking for the elevator, lingers. Descending from above, the elevator car sent him tumbling to the basement from the fourth floor. He was, they say, a happy man, happy to have escaped bullets or gangrene in the Great War, happy to be working on the building of the most sumptuous hotel in Calgary in 1913, happy to have died such a quick and memorable death. His ghost is unremarkable, a quiet draft that fails to raise the hair on the back of my neck, although I would be happy to do a quick fox-trot with him across the lobby.

Robert Barr's ghost enjoys the repeated declaration that there are no ghosts in the Palliser. He tells that story to the tradespeople and repairmen that come and go in the daily maintenance of this huge pile of a building. "No ghosts here," he says, chuckling. "No hauntings." And they wonder at his old-fashioned clothes before they proceed with their tool kits and their duct tape, mending the continuous small chips and leaks of a well-used building.

I think of the bellhop being questioned tomorrow by the police.

"Did she seem uneasy?" they will ask. "Did she know the

man she was meeting? Did you notice anything unusual? How did she behave?"

Their questions undertowing his bewilderment that one of the guests he has ushered toward a good night's sleep has betrayed him by refusing to practice the ritual of rising, dressing, breakfast, check-out.

I feel oddly smug about this premeditated morning, as if for once I know more than a hotel staff member, as though by planning to surprise him, I have broken a taboo, swished behind those doors marked Employees Only.

But that's not fair. He is pleasant, smiling despite a rash of acne across his forehead. He wears a discreet gold hoop in his left ear. How young are bellhops? And is his job temporary, or does he want to lug luggage from lobby to guest room for the rest of his life?

"Having a good day?" I ask, inanely. Really, I don't want to talk to him, but some perverse part of my socialized past makes me want him to remember me, smiling, my demeanor pleasant and calm.

"Yes, ma'am. Looks like the chinook is on its way."

"The wind."

He grins and I know what he's thinking. The chinook makes the city turn wanton. If it were possible to hear over the rush of wild air, the cries of pleasure on chinook nights would be measurably amplified. He's probably planning his own escape once he's killed his shift.

So he won't be working tomorrow morning when they discover me, although they will certainly question him. He's more attentive than the desk clerk; he'll be able to offer a description, a few specific observations. On the other hand, they might not discover me in the morning—it could be after-noon or evening, or even the following day.

How will my accomplice depart? Will he put the Do Not

Disturb sign on the doorknob, will he contrive to lock the door so that the maid can't enter? But it's no concern of mine. I'll be in another country.

The elevator bell tings, and the bellhop motions for me to step out. "Here we are."

Those words, that gesture. I've heard them over and over, in so many countries, as different from one another as milk and meat, a global traveler's ritual. We turn left and walk down the hall to the bottom leg of the hotel's E-shape, and I feel a cramp of desire, wet between my legs as sudden and unexpected as pain.

"Have you stayed with us before?" asks the bellhop.

I can only mutter that yes, yes, I have. Some time ago, but I have.

⁓

I ARGUE WITH my dear one. "What matters," I say to him, "are private hopes, dreams without guilt, duty, defection."

"Bullshit," he says, stroking the back of my neck. "What matters are carrots, venetian blinds, toboggans, a glass of cold water."

He's like that, my dear one.

⁓

YES, I DID stay here, once, many years ago.

Staring at the blurred rectangle of the window, I lay awake, my chest clenched and aching. It is a strange feeling to lie in an impersonal hotel bed trying to control your weeping, trying to keep yourself from shouting with sobs, fearful that the body beside you will wake and demand explanations. Crying is an act that the world expects us to keep secret, behind closed curtains and locked doors, as if it were an indulgence.

The light that rose from the street below glowed green, shone against the frame of the bathroom door, still half-open, cut across the solid rectangle of the bed. That was back when the Palliser had steam radiators; they gurgled and hissed a language all their own, as if the voices of all those who had slept there were murmuring.

I wanted to die.

My wanting to die was part of a conversation that I never had with that particular assassin or with any of the assassins that followed him. None of them asked, not one noticed or registered any passion beyond the usual ampersand of bodies, as if genital conjunction should be enough to still all tears. Unprofessional assassins want to believe that decisions of desire are accidental, unplanned, not their responsibility. They believe a woman makes herself available because she's there. Unprofessional assassins believe that women need them, and they are remarkably oblivious to what our bodies crave.

The first time I stayed here I was green. I was with an unprofessional assassin, blundering, oblivious. He assumed that women loved fulfilling needs, having somehow authored the casserole waiting in the oven, the ironed and folded stack of handkerchiefs in the drawer, the brisk relief of intercourse. And yet he could not imagine that another person might have reciprocal needs. He'd forgotten condoms—no, he hadn't forgotten, just didn't bother to bring them, as if only I were responsible, and he even took my toothbrush, slid a lump of my paste on its bristles and energetically brushed his malignantly square teeth.

He did not want to hear my crying. He did not want to know why I wanted to die. He slept and I lay awake, watching the wash of city light swirl over the walls, hearing the late night grind of the one o'clock freight on the tracks behind the hotel. Imagining the rest of my life in a disentanglement of utilitarian limbs, the word *love* to be avoided at all costs, the body recalcitrant in its longing, bone-lonely for a hand to stroke my head until my eyes closed in sleep.

I wanted to die, and not one of those assassins ever noticed. Although, of course, they all wanted to kill me.

THE DOOR TO Room 531 is not ajar, but emphatically closed.

"Perhaps he's gone out," I say, sounding foolish.

The bellhop puts my bag down, knocks, waits with his head cocked. When there is no reply, he inserts the key, pushes open this portal to the last room I will know on earth.

"After you."

I enter cautiously. I have made the arrangements, I know the outline of events, but the details could still surprise me, catch me off guard. I do not relish surprises, a strange man jumping out at me, the sudden rush of physical contact.

The room is empty, profoundly so, as if waiting for confirmation. Such a plain room, tasteful, replete with tempered comfort and yet restraint. The bellhop switches on the lights, extracts the luggage rack from the closet, rests my garment bag there, a fat clutch waiting to be folded apart. He opens the doors to the console, clicks on the television, pushes wide the bathroom door.

"Anything else you might need? Ice? Room service?"

"No thanks." I slide a five dollar bill into his hand. Two dollars a bag is the norm. I should send him off with a two dollar coin, but what use will I have for money after tonight? And it feels good to see him smile, even blush a little, as if I have tipped him for his charm. He turns toward the door, hesitates with the knob still in his hand, then makes an almost ceremonial bow and goes, pulling the door behind him.

I could have laid him on the edge of the bed. I know the unspoken gestures that concede that possibility, and I have even taken advantage of such lonely ragtag moments. In Stockholm, in Berlin, in Moose Jaw.

Not today. Although the room is empty, there's no telling when my Mr. Atman will appear. He has already been here. In the closet is a compact black flight bag, the kind you can wheel onto airplanes and stow under the seat in front of you.

I stand in front of the open closet door, staring. The bag is scuffed and well used, not ominous but cozy. I reach to touch it, yes, I know, I am supposed to want to open it, snoop into my own demise, but I am sadly incurious, not willing to discover ropes or syringes, silk fetters or silencer attachments. I close the closet door and walk to the window.

Across the way I can see into another room, the E of the hotel's Chicago-style wings reflecting windows toward one another. A woman is standing beside the bed in her room, pulling on a pair of tights. She bends from the waist, absorbed in her encasement, stretching the legs as she eases the stockings up. I am certain I see her smile toward her toes, which she inserts into high-heeled pumps before settling a long skirt over her head and zipping it snug at the waist.

I flop onto the bed without taking off my shoes, lie on my back with my hands behind my head and stare at the neatly plastered ceiling.

HERE, NO ONE knows me.

Avoiding recognition is one of travel's seductions. Travel enables that shift to an anonymous world, where you can kiss publicly and never be observed, where you can faint and not wake humiliated, where you can sit at a café table and read without fear of recognition or interruption, having escaped the density of a place that harbors the habits worn into days and weeks, time spun inward.

That is why I traveled, to compose a private self and give her the space to breathe.

THE TROUBLE IS, I thought I was anonymous, but someone always recognized me, stopped me on the street to ask if I was not the woman they saw buying cakes in Vienna yesterday, and although I knew I was that same woman, although I remembered seeing them at a table next to me in Demel's, where I sat and watched the *demelerinnen*'s shoes, slashed open over their impending bunions, I denied my previous entendre, pretended that I was in Budapest and couldn't possibly have been contemplating cream tarts in Konditorei Demel.

So much for the privacies of restlessness.

Found out.

TRAVELING IS A conversation with elusive minutes, time zones destroying simultaneous life. Sir Sandford Fleming wanted the arrival and departure of trains to be predictable.

Every traveler knows the strange hours that movement keeps. Through the act of traveling, time takes on a new tense, a different country. Time acts as bribery for diffidence, a text of unbecoming, something shaken loose from the gravel of settled bones and dictatorial schedules, rising and lying down, alarm and hunger.

The panoply of time zones, those invisible lines that make the sun follow its sphere, insist on separation, inscribe loss. And horizontal lines, the Tropic of Capricorn, the Arctic Circle, the 49th parallel, all of them are ominous in their homage to Mercator. Time holds us fast, makes us believe that we can pace ourselves within its relentless continuance. Caught by those tentacles, we imagine that we can escape the scanty designation of tourist and become someone different, a person able to occupy another time and place.

But like dogs we carry innate time within us, wake at unusual hours and then long to curl up and nap in the middle of a carpeted museum. The body refuses to be tricked by sunlight or the rattle of morning teacups, becomes voyeur rather than participant, resisting and demanding, dragging its feet from square to square, fidgeting intemperately throughout some solemn guided tour or speech. If time were simultaneous, the eyes staring at Coronation Square or the Brandenberg Gate could be transplanted to the icy dawn of revolution, the coup, the uprising, a moment inescapable, destined to be repeated. To be present but invisible is every traveler's desire, and yet that very invisibility is the crux of traveling's voyeurism.

I want my dear one to be going to bed when I do, not six hours later, my sleep already over before his has begun, so that waking alone at ten in the morning, I am bereft because I cannot call him because it is three and I would disturb his time with my own. Awake while my lover sleeps. He wakeful while I sleep. A restless disconnection.

I try to imagine my dear one at work in the hospital, edging from bed to bed to bed, his hand on a child's arm, his ear turned to a request. I try to imagine him driving through a yellow light or buying a newspaper, but the effort makes me stumble, and I'm the one warped by time, unable to step around what is so casually called jet lag.

⌒◯

IF DESTINATION WERE some simultaneous time zone that could hold two people together even when they are in different places, everyone would want to go there. The Concorde would be over-booked.

I am arranging such a destination now.

⌒◯

RESTLESSNESS SETTLES ON the heart like dust, works its way into the cracks of a life's tempo so stealthily that time begins to shriek and warp, movement becomes a respiratory resolve.

Restlessness crouches inside suitcases that fold themselves against the air of basements, waiting for their mouths to gape, that waft of patience, the valise, vagina, *valigia*, vigilant as the dark air of waiting to arrive, the singe of breath in a new place. As if privacy could be held in the clasp of a bag, its lock and straps, its solid bodkin and bustling manner, the bruises on its corner knuckles honestly won.

Travelers believe that our secret selves are kept safe by the rotund zipper of a suitcase, the tight click of metal snap. That is why we hover so anxiously at the baggage belts, waiting for the rubber to start its swishing circle. That is why we rush to haul at the handles of our luggage, pull it into our arms. Something precious in that bag we have packed, something peculiar to ourselves in the arrangement of underwear and socks, folded trousers and dovetailed shirts.

The truth is that all luggage is interchangeable. We could pick up any suitcase from that carousel and find enough of what is needed. The size might not be perfect, but the idea would be sufficient, an imaginary outfitting.

Portmanteau could be the name of a perfume, a book, even an hourglass. It lurks suggestively, a mantle, a portal. But closed.

MY LUGGAGE WAS once delayed at Heathrow and did not appear when I landed in Madrid. As is customary, they agreed to deliver the suitcase when it arrived, and a day later a courtesy van brought it to my hotel.

It was my bag all right. No mistake. Nothing was missing. But they had added to it, neatly tucked in someone else's surely missing things. A pair of horn-rimmed reading glasses, which I don't need. A leather-cased stainless steel pen of an expensive make. A Swiss army knife. A map of Toronto.

Well, after all, I am Canadian.

BECAUSE I AM a professional traveler, the expectation is that I have learned to jump onto planes without accoutrements, that I travel light.

In fact, I carry far too much, overpack gleefully.

I could pretend that such irrational conduct stems from a trip to Belgium one late November, the streets of Brussels elegantly decorated with pine boughs, the skies bristling with frost, cold so fierce not all the chocolate in the city could thaw my bones. I came back to the hotel after delivering a set of blueprints and sat on the edge of the tub, my feet in boiling water, trying to warm them toward a semisolid state.

My dear one did not answer the phone.

Now I overpack, although I still don't dress warmly enough.

THE SUITCASE DISEASE has grown in me with age.

I turn into leather shops and measure the sides of bags as if I need something special to transport a french horn, a violin of clothes. I prod shoe pouches to see whether they can stretch to hold boots. I insist on certain zipper weights, expandable side pockets, inner belts that will compress clothes to their thinnest fiber. I buy more suitcases than I can ever carry, have left behind more valises than I will ever need.

They were a tax deduction.

HERE IS THE burden of my argument with life.

I have forgotten homesickness.

I HAVE AT last come to the moment when I will be able to apprehend myself elsewhere. That idea is straight out of *Dog Sleeps*, my last good read, not yet unpacked.

Unable to apprehend myself, I admit to my evasions, my continuing journeys, as acts of self-trickery. I have always believed that I will apprehend myself elsewhere, for at home I am evasive as a veil.

Pilgrim, I look for the houses of those who managed to scratch their names in the stone of time. I wait for the streets to cry out, to tell me that Christina Rossetti walked here, or even a woman like me, terrified and alone, weeping silently behind her hands.

Traveling convinces me that I will be lucky enough to stumble over my own feet as I round a corner, as I elbow my way through a crowded bar to order a gin and tonic with ice and lemon.

The woman standing there, face tilted slightly away, hair shading her eyes, will be me, finally apprehended, and willing to be found. Eager to recognize herself. At last.

WHAT IS THE source of restlessness? A guilty heart. Trembling legs. An impatience with toast crumbs and flossing. A glass of water drunk too quickly. A terrible conscience. The second hand on the kitchen clock. Not the first gray hair but the third. Shoes that are too big. Longing. Shoes that are too small. Staying home.

A KEY TURNS in the lock. My assassin arrives.

HE IS NOT late. It is impossible to be late or early for such an assignation. He has merely arrived, entering the room I have chosen as my life's caboose.

I sit up guiltily. I've had my street shoes on the spread.

He comes through the envelope of the door as comfortably as if he were my longtime companion. Practiced.

I swing my legs over the side of the bed, perch there, my blood hammering in my wrists. He does not need to tell me who he is. He fits the description I have invented for myself, a man who looks rather like Bruno Ganz in *Wings of Desire*.

"I went out to have a cup of coffee. I hope you weren't waiting long." He does not reach to touch me, the enforced civility of shaking hands, but smiles, and his face lights with the spare beauty of a portrait saint.

"No, only a few moments." I do not need to introduce myself.

He shrugs off his overcoat and steps around my bag, still hunched unopened on the luggage rack, to hang the coat in the closet. "A wonderful afternoon out there. That exhilarating wind."

He does not sound like he is making small talk or stating what is obviously banal. He makes the chinook wind glorious, an orchestra or a character in a play. I should not be surprised at the raspy sexiness of his voice. After all, he is a version of seducer.

He stops then, in the short space between the closet and the bed, his body held as though for my inspection. These are the rules. If there is anything about him that I find repulsive, I can terminate the process. I will still have to pay the kill fee, but in such circumstances, the notion of going forward merely in order to save money is crazy.

He tells me, as he is required to, that I can change my mind right up until he commits the act and finishes what I have initiated.

I nod, and he too eases down on the edge of the bed, not close to me, but close to my posture, the two of us caught in uncomfortable pause.

He is dressed conventionally enough in a pair of black trousers, a narrow-striped and well-pressed shirt buttoned at the throat, although no tie, under a jacket that is a mix of wool, possibly cashmere in the blend. The body beneath the clothes is solid but not fat, no arrogant belly, no heavy thighs. His strength is in his flexibility, his attentiveness. He appears to occupy that ubiquitous middle age somewhere between forty-six and fifty-nine, his face saddened by creases around

the eyes and the mouth, but not aged toward stone, not yet finished. He wears copper-rimmed glasses. His hair has thinned,
but he's cut it short so it does not suggest the greasy luster of
balding men who cling to their few remaining strands.

His is a face worth trusting.

He is wearing gloves.

I am at last alone in a room with a man who wears gloves
for a living.

BETWEEN DEPARTURE AND arrival I am desolate, inconsolable.
With every embarkation, I want to be back home, waiting for
light to filter the blinds, the cool mountain air to drift heavier
and heavier as the morning stirs and my garden waters itself
with the dark's dew. Waiting for my dear one to stir and curl
himself around me.

Here, now, waiting to arrive at the moment of ultimate
arrival, ultimate departure, I want to weep into my hands,
homesick for my own terrible restlessness and its demise, its
closed confusion.

I want to weep, but then he will have to comfort me. This
is my assassin; I don't want to compromise his contract.

I SUPPOSE IT'S up to me to speak. I turn toward him, then
can't think of what to say, although I sense that he is as
nervous as I am.

"Will you take a more comfortable seat?"

"Thanks," he says, and gets up, moves around the bed toward the armchair next to the window. He knows I am stalling, that I do not want him to see me break down, betraying my own betrayal. He must remain neutral, show neither impatience nor surprise, do as I ask.

I THINK IRRATIONALLY that this too is a foreign place—"just one of the many places that would be different if you were a part of it." *Dog Sleeps* again, lurking in my head as well as my suitcase.

Places aren't foreign if we're a part of them. We domesticate our landmarks, name the bicycle store on the southwest corner of the street, the gas station that offers free cereal with a fill, the lilacs blooming in Riley Park.

Is that why I resist the next destination? Longing to be connected again, different times and places helping me to avoid the griefs knotted hard as ingots under my pillow, waiting for me to open my eyes and resist the amnesia of dreaming.

My dear one does not let me dream. When I cry out, he rests his hand on my shoulder, strokes my head until I wake and fall asleep again.

DID ONLY JOURNEYS on airplanes and trains permit me to stand beside myself? I am truly beside myself now, cannot seem to merge with whomever that self is named, if she is different from who she once was or wanted to be.

I have convinced myself that I am happiest striding down the long corridors that lead to train platforms, that signal boarding gates or departing ferries. Bent slightly with the weight of a briefcase, I watch myself walking toward a destination, convinced that the transition suggests an answer, if not an exaggeration.

SILHOUETTED IN THE armchair by the window, his face is shadowed against the failing light. Turned sideways on the bed, my knee bent, although now I carefully keep my shoes from the cover, I study him, the sadness around his eyes meeting mine.

I have to break the ice, maybe even try a joke. "Wouldn't you rather do this in a park?" I ask. "A hotel room seems so enclosed, confined." I'm almost serious, but find I am enjoying this, the polite boundaries usually in place between people absent. "Or perhaps a more appropriate setting, like a graveyard?" This is hilarious.

"It's too risky. Someone would see us."

Of course. To grave one needs a fine and private place.

I rise, walk around the bed to the armchair on the other side of the window. As I pass, I look across to the room opposite, hoping to glimpse the woman, now invisible, who was so carefully sliding her tights up the length of her thighs. I sit cornered to Derrick Atman, the two of us companions in front of a fire, except there is no fire, only the window framed by striped drapes, outside a Calgary wind blowing winter leaves, the sky leaden with the change in air pressure and temperature.

He smiles, and I look for the false pull of mouth muscle that liars smile with, their eyes cold as hail. I am shocked to see that he means it, his smile takes me in, pays attention, when I incline my head he follows, when I move my hands he notices. Of course, he has to be good at this, he has to inspire trust in me, his incipient victim. I hesitate. Surely a professional would avoid connection, would offer cold-cut smiles and dead responses. Is it easier to kill someone you know or to kill someone that you know nothing about? Is it easier to stop the breath of a person or a cipher? I've always thought it must be simpler to kill a stranger. Wrong, I realize now, with a terribly clarity. The more knowledge between the killer and killee, the less deliberate the kill can be. Does this killer require meaning in order to act?

"Well."

"Well?"

Far below I can hear traffic's faint grind, the wind swirling between that mechanical rush. The afternoon out there will be winding down, rush hour traffic sliding across one-way streets, every car a homing pigeon with its human cargo destined for the news on television, dinner, maybe a movie, reports to read, then sleep, a dream faintly tattooed by the knocking wind's warm breath.

Does everyone, I wonder, sleep the way I do, with my window flung wide to frost and wind and showers, burrowed under two duvets to keep warm but open always to Calgary's sweet weather?

I get up, bend toward the window, and yes, it is old-fashioned enough to have a latch, handles; it can be opened. I pull it up so a gust of wind bells the curtains, shouts into the room. "That's the worst thing about most hotel rooms," I say. "You can't open the windows."

43

"You like fresh air." He makes this sound like a complexity he has discovered, not an obvious statement, painting my breathing larger than it is, bending toward me with an energy green with hope.

"Yes, I miss the prairie air when I am away."

"Do you go away often then?"

"Often enough. My job takes me away—"

I hesitate at my own description, how much I want to reveal. But what can he do with this information after his job is complete? Nothing except avoid accusation.

"I travel a great deal," I admit.

"Most people would consider you lucky. Everyone wants to travel."

"Yes, that's the popular misconception, that travel is desirable, fun, exotic."

"I gather you conceive differently."

I nod at him, again a catch in my throat, feeling sorry for myself and my footloose life. But I refuse to cry when we've barely been in this room for half an hour. And I'm cautious. He sees too quickly, with an instinct clairvoyants pray for. I lean against the window, swallow, wait for my eyes to clear.

"People long for what they have never done," he says softly. "Tell me, what do you do?"

I RUN AWAY. I play hide and seek. I practice kinematics.

I LOOK FOR innovative ecstasies, ways of coming home, ways of decamping, ways to abandon the scene of uncommitted crimes.

Rootless. Castaway. Robinson Crusoe without an island, and certainly never with a Friday, eager to break the monotony.

I TRAVEL IN order to entertain quiescence.

"Do I HAVE to answer your questions?"

"Of course not. You don't have to tell me anything."

"Why do you ask? Wouldn't you rather keep me at arm's length?"

"I'm a curious man. I like to know a little about the people I assist."

"And what if I ask you questions?"

"I'll answer them."

Aha. Not, I'll *try* to answer them. And his body, comfortable in the armchair, one leg flung across the other, his loafers polished, his socks an elegant black, convinces me. I'm shocked to realize that he isn't lying.

"Okay," I begin lamely, "what's your name?"

"You know my name. Derrick Atman."

"Where do you live?"

"Winnipeg."

"Winnipeg?"

"Yes, Winnipeg."

I eye him skeptically. I imagined him coming from else-where, an expert flying into town, completing this contract, flying off again, but not to Winnipeg. Dallas or New York maybe—surely professional assassins come from cities with a gun permit. Instead, he seems the reverse of me, and with a naive address. "You've brought a suitcase."

"So have you."

"It seems necessary when a person checks into a hotel."

"Exactly."

I have to chuckle. He hasn't got the deafness follicle, the oblivion gene that my other assassins used as an excuse. Why did I imagine that he would echo their indifference? If he did, he would not be the perfect assassin.

"Shall we unpack then?" I ask, quite gaily. "I'd like to brush my teeth."

THE JOB OF A courier is to bring together disjointed parts, to triangulate the previously unconnected. Whatever I carry—a sheaf of paper, a computer disc, perhaps even a sample of a product, cloth or plastic, or a newly concocted drug—that item becomes the transition point of a triangle between sender and receiver.

Such deliveries are futuristic acts, although no one now knows what futurism is or what futurism stands for. It has been let out of the dictionaries.

"I thought," he says, rising from his chair, "that futurism was associated with virility."

He's reading my mind. "That too," I say. "That too."

~⟨⟩~

"AND HOW DID you train for such a particular job?"

"Train? Pure repetition, each completed delivery enhanced my reputation."

"So reputation is the key?"

"Isn't it important for your work too?"

"No, mine requires precision."

"It's like I'm a reliable mail-room clerk. People are careless, you know. They forget things, they drop them, they jam them into overhead luggage compartments, all kinds of odd neglects and absentmindedness. If the package is sensitive, and it most often is, neither sender nor receiver likes the thought of it being committed to distracted postal clerks or nerve-jangled truck drivers or sweating baggage handlers. Nobody wants to send a valuable item, whether dirt samples or diamonds, through the general system."

"So you carry precious items from one place to another."

"Right. And I'm scrupulously consistent, always on time, never a package damaged or tampered with, I'm good with customs officials, meticulous with forms. I've never screwed up a delivery."

"Never."

"Never. That's why I'm a top-of-the-line courier. I started with smaller things that needed to be hand delivered, and because I was so reliable, I got more and more sensitive material."

47

"No contraband?"

"Absolutely not."

"Not even tempted?" He opens the closet door, bends toward his bag tucked there.

"That would be the end. A courier is marked anyway; we're watched, checked all the time. If I were ever to step past the legal line, I would be in jail in a minute."

"And you are never curious, never think of opening one of the packages to see for yourself if the computer disc is green or blue or if the diamonds are real?"

"Here, you have the luggage rack." I lift my bag and toss it onto the bed. "No, I mail my curiosity to other destinations."

He unzips his bag, lifts the flap.

I refuse to peer, bend attentively over my own zipper, but my body is stiff with peripheral watching.

"Come here then," he says, and when I turn he is holding both gloved hands toward me in a gesture of supplication.

"What?" I move to stand beside him, and we both look down at his open bag.

"See, nothing sinister."

I register a neatly folded shirt, a compact toilet kit. Nothing sinister, no terrible instruments. But of course a skillful killer uses what's at hand, an innocent razor, a convenient pair of fine dernier panty hose.

He lifts a blue cable-knit sweater and walks toward the dresser. "I like to put a few things in the drawers, make the room feel more personal."

"Do you do this often then?" It's late for me to raise the question I might have dared to ask earlier.

"Only on request." His answer is steady but soft.

I'm ashamed. I've set this up, hired him to participate, insisted on him as accomplice. I know I'm paying, but still I don't need to be sarcastic. "Sorry." I look into my own suitcase. I've brought three changes of clothes, although I cannot imagine why. It seemed necessary to have with me clean underwear, a dress, a different shirt and trousers. Perhaps after I have been killed, he will dress me, conceal my demise with a fresh costume.

"Don't be sorry. My job is like yours, necessary but unrecognized. Although yours beats mine hands down for pleasure."

"I don't think of it as such a wonderful job. I'm always on airplanes or trains, and modern transportation is boring, boring. I get to spend about three days in some of the most beautiful and famous cities of the world, but I always have to leave again."

"Other people would kill for it."

"Ha, I tried for years to kill myself. I've had to admit defeat and hire a professional."

He chuckles. Carrying his shaving kit into the bathroom, a middle-aged man contracted to eliminate my vital signs, he chuckles, and midway through hanging my silk shirt on a hanger, I have to catch myself, interrupt a gasp. I am comfortable with him as I have never been with a stranger, here in this hotel room. I am almost as comfortable with him as I am with my dear one, my dear one dancing me around the kitchen, my dear one, my dear one splashing the soap from my back in the shower.

I am almost happy.

WHAT IS CARRIED in the maw of an experienced suitcase is a paraleipsis. Not to mention what else might come along for the trip.

I'VE USED EVERY conceivable kind of suitcase. Now I use the standard roller bag, compact enough to pull down the aisle of an airplane, snug enough to tuck under the seat in front of me. Able to contain an amazing amount, changes of underwear that insist on their own repetition, as if sanity can be maintained by a pair of clean panties.

I'm less fond of that practical bag than I am of my old suitcases, those molded lozenges of cardboard and plastic, even an old leather portmanteau, the corners scuffed, and the finish starting to flake. I love its buckles, its sense of humor. One of the corner reinforcement caps is gone, which makes it look rakish, but that suitcase talked to me, could tell me what the flight was like, how often the train was cleaned, whether the sky would pour down rain. It was heavy, though, cumbersome, and I gave it up for a tough little synthetic jeep bag that could have survived being run over by a backhoe. Until I moved up to the clinical aluminum and plastic-wheeled job that I unpacked the day before yesterday.

Now I'm left with this last suitcase, a beautiful oxblood garment bag, even my initials engraved on the clasp, and containing only the few things I need for closing night.

DOG SLEEPS RESTS amid my clothes, a book with a warm sepia cover.

I flip it open, read aloud, "'Home is always something taken from the dresser.'"

"Home?"

"Don't you think that's accurate? What is home but something that we take along, retrieved from a dresser or pulled from a closet. Isn't putting your sweater in the drawer here an affirmation of hominess?"

"Or," and now he grins, "maybe dresser drawers are smart like thieves, vigilant, wary, antidotes to vacancy. Signs and warnings."

"So we fill them? Counterbalance the drift of aimlessness by the countable numbers of socks and underwear that accompany us, even if we wash the same garment out in the sink every night, hang it to dry over a hotel room radiator?"

"Well, people surely feel that drawers and cupboards, hangers and glasses, are meant to be—used."

"Occupied?"

"That too."

"You mean as an antidote to the sprinkler star on the ceiling, the standard-sized towels, the heavy drapes."

"Sure, a way to claim space. Or leave a message. You must have found forgotten items in hotel room drawers."

I frown, thinking. "Oh sure, all kinds of things. Imagine what the maids discover. I've accidentally left behind my favorite red silk brassiere, a pair of hand-painted slacks, a bottle of exquisite Spanish brandy that I intended to savor. More hair dryers than I can count, and only too many earrings and knee-highs."

"But you're listing what you remember leaving. What about those items that you don't know you left, that you've actually forgotten?"

"I found a box of polished stones once. A packet of ribbed condoms, a purple curly ribbon wrapped around the outside. Matches from completely different restaurants in different cities. The Criterion. Janos. Giorgio's. An undeveloped film."

"Did you get it printed?"

"I felt sneaky. I took the roll home when I should have turned it in to the hotel's lost and found."

"What did the pictures tell you?"

"They were photographs of someone's dog, all kinds of poses of a smiling golden retriever."

"No people?"

I shake my head. "No people. Just the dog, sitting, running, eating from his bowl. Do you have a dog?"

"No, no dog."

"Children?"

"Two. Grown up now. At university down east."

"A wife?"

"Yes, a wife."

"Does she know?"

He shakes his head. "She can't know."

"So—" A light blinks yellow in the room across the way, and I realize that the afternoon is growing dark. The woman who was pulling on her tights drops her coat on the bed, seems to be searching for something on the desk. I'm watching her while I ask, "So—you can only talk about your work with the people you—"

"With my companions. Exactly."

THE FIRST IMPULSE of a hotel dresser drawer is the vapor that rises when it's opened. I have bent my nose to sandalwood, smoke, mustiness, brown sugar, lemon verbena, coffee beans, sprigs of lavender, a woman's silk underpants soaked with desire.

In old hotels the drawers often stick, need to be wrenched open, as if they're resisting years of sliding, decades of enfoldment. In modern hotels drawers are silent, on casters, limited in number. Each room can bear only three drawers, three brief and paper-lined drawers ready to accommodate whatever can't be hung in the closet.

There are bold eccentric drawers, like the room in Berlin lined on every side with drawers, drawers crawling up the wall to the ceiling, all functional, all empty, the highest impossible to reach despite their alluring knobs. The room did not supply a ladder. Or there are secret drawers requiring a search for the hidden catch release in order to open them. On one, the catch relocated itself so that after I had put a good red tricot away, I could not spring it from its secure location, and was forced to leave it behind. Then there are drawers that are not drawers but handles affixed to a blank piece of wood, façades without compartments, drawers without three-dimensional space.

I have given up expecting drawers to be erotic, and now expect them to be domestic.

WHAT IS TROUBLING about hotels is that life can be reduced to a bed, a lamp, a table, a closet, a sink, the gestures of the body reduced to acts of maintenance.

Before I unpack, I hunt through closets and drawers, open every door and window, try every key. And yet there is always a door I miss, connective, mysterious, a gateway to a different room. There is always a drawer I have failed to pull open, a drawer that holds an expired cockroach or a secret message scrawled in a language I do not read. Once again I fail to make the connection.

～✍

"THERE ARE NEVER enough hangers in hotel rooms." I rattle the six ranked on the closet rail.

"Well, you take along more clothing than most people do for a single night."

I glance at him quickly, suspecting sarcasm or male arrogance. He's teasing me, that I can tell, but tenderly, without sting. I decide to answer him straight, let him do what he wants with the information.

"Probably. It's habit because I can't bear the airplane smell that permeates my clothes after I've been sitting on a flight. It must be the air or the disinfectant they spray planes with. So I have to have enough clothes to change completely, every time."

"There is such a thing as sending them out to a laundry."

"No, laundries are terrible. They shrink everything or send back somebody else's shirts. I would rather wash them myself, even in a sink, with a packet of travel suds."

"And what about drying them?"

"Oh, I drape everything over the shower bar. And pray for an iron."

THE BELLS OF Knox United begin to toll. I count. Six o'clock. Dark streams past the window now, and wisps of what looks like fine rain. Or is it the wind itself, the chinook made visible?

"Six o'clock," I say.

He shrugs. "We have all night."

ONE OF MY habits is trying to decipher the patterns of bells. In some cities and villages they ring every quarter, in some every half, some only every hour. The intricate conversation of peeling bells reminds me of my dear one, the bell of his alarm clock before he leaves for the hospital. We never have all night.

Bells seem to speak a language that I have missed, and they are all calling to me, "Stranger, go home."

I WANT TO accept Derrick Atman's pacing as his own, his gentle mockery as liking, but I feel compelled to be suspicious.

I narrow my eyes at him. "Are you supposed to try and make me change my mind?"

"I am supposed to give you every possible opportunity to decide. Finally."

"And when I say, you will proceed."

"Yes. But we do have all night. Neither one of us needs to

55

be somewhere else. The room is paid for. We don't have a deadline."

BUT I DO. I've been traveling for years. I want to arrive.

Every person wishes for a subtle assassin, the natural magic of a perfectly arranged end. And doesn't it make sense that people want to determine their final moments—at the same time denying death, avoiding it even when crumbling bodies yearn for sleep.

Why should death be arbitrary, unplanned? A lightning bolt. A sudden swerve of the automobile into a concrete abutment. Or a gradual weakening, so imperceptible that time disappears.

What could efficiently cause my death, my having made nothing of my life but mechanical connections? Airplanes don't crash that often.

And my work isn't hazardous. I merely carry things from one place to another, ensure that the right person has signed for the package or the envelope, that I am paid. A courier only slightly upscale from the bicycle boys who ply their legs through the downtown streets, doing in essence the same job. All I need is a pillbox hat and a bell. What is my purpose but that filled by a pander, a go-between, connecting programs or formulae, messages of presumed importance? Delivery girl, all my life's urgency has come from without, and for once, for once, I want to be in charge of my own conclusions, my own delivery. Is that an act of hubris?

I'm not afraid of what death will bring. People recoil from unimaginable ideas, find them abhorrent, but death seems to me as sweet as a vanilla candle, as heliotrope as the sun itself.

⌒

"TOMORROW WOULD BE a good day to travel," Derrick Atman says.

"And the day after better yet. I'm finished traveling."

"You might miss traveling."

"You're trying to dissuade me."

"Never."

We've unpacked, ground to a halt. What happens now? Do I say to him, "All right, go ahead"? Do I wait for him to make suggestions? I remember that I have to sign something, a contract or a disclaimer form, a manifest. He's gone back to his chair by the window, his head tipped against his gloved hand, relaxed. He looks almost sleepy.

I take my toiletries bag into the bathroom and hang it on the hook behind the door. I brush my teeth, gently, thoroughly, floss, then wash my face and brush my hair. I stare at the mirror, meeting my own eyes.

In all my years of traveling, I've never felt so certainly arrived. I am alone in a hotel room with my killer. At last.

⌒

THIS KILLER ISN'T a gasbag. I'll give him that. When I want silence, he senses it, stays quiet.

My other assassins were talkers, muttering under their

breath, grinding their teeth, stating the obvious—pointing out to me that it was raining, that the train was late, that poisonous people love poison. All observations I could make myself. And they were clumsy, overturning water glasses, stepping on my heels, bumping into me, eager to snatch an elbow, quick to suggest unspecified intercourse. "Let's do it here," until I started answering automatically, "Do what?"

Except for my dear one, a quiet man who speaks with his eyes, his hands gentle, without grasping, never wanting to possess. When he first touched my head, I flinched, nervous.

"You don't like your head being touched."

"No."

His hand on my neck was light, tender with reassurance, as if to offer me angelic cognitions. My dear one.

⁓

THE PHONE RINGS.

I step out of the bathroom and stare at it.

It rings and rings again, loud, accusatory.

Derrick Atman walks around the bed, snatches it from its cradle. "Yes?"

"_____"

"Oh, thank you."

"_____"

"Fine." He puts the receiver down.

I'm furious, enraged that the shimmering block of the room's isolation has been invaded, the dimness made electronic, the calm stitches between me and my killer unraveling.

"I'm sorry," he says, shaking his head.

"What? What the hell was that?"

"The front desk."

"The front desk!"

"Wanting to deliver something."

"Deliver something? Is this part of your method?"

"No, it is not part of my method. I'm sorry. I didn't expect to be interrupted. Look, it's partly the noise that's surprised us. I'll turn the phone down."

"What the hell?"

"Apparently," he says, the phone upside down in his hand, just as there is a knock at the door, "apparently—"

He clicks the phone volume button a notch lower, goes to the door, opens it to a plastic-ballooned spear of tiger lilies, which he takes, thanking the deliverer and easing the door shut with his foot. "Apparently, I am considered a valued customer, and they send valued customers bouquets of flowers."

I've backed into the corner, can feel my face snarling.

"Truly," he tears the plastic from the flowers, clumsily because of his gloves, sets the arrangement on top of the television console, where it blooms orange and sticky. "This is not usual. I am sorry."

"Valued customer?"

"Look, it's a hotel invention. Every day they order a half-dozen bouquets. If, by six o'clock, there aren't enough vips who merit flowers in their rooms, they just send them to whomever they think will appreciate them. They probably checked the register and my name looked vaguely familiar."

"You're tricking me. They know you. You're going to turn me in, call an ambulance, a suicide hotline; you have no intention of carrying this job out."

"I do not sabotage assignments."

"You agreed that you would kill me." I can feel my voice

ready to burst into tears. This arrangement began so auspiciously, and now the glass has cracked.

"Oh," he says dryly, returning to his chair. "I will. I will."

THE ADVANTAGE OF a hotel is that everyone is supposed to be incognito.

I AM FURIOUS, shaken. I glare at him, although he does not fumble with justifications and explanations, only spreads his gloved hands in that odd gesture of supplication, and waits.

"How can I believe you?"

"You can't. You have to trust me, you've had to trust me from the moment you chose to set up this meeting, from the moment that we walked through the door."

AT LEAST HE doesn't tell me to calm down, but sits quietly, then says, "Surely you didn't think that we could proceed without any interruption, without one accidental encounter or unplanned person on the periphery?"

I sit on the edge of the bed again, cover my face with my

hands. I will not cry. I will not cry. I'm crying. Eventually the room grows darker. I lift my head.

His eyes are closed. He has taken his glasses off and holds them in his gloved left hand. Across the wing, the woman in the room opposite is sitting at the desk in a pool of light, writing. Her hand dashes across the page. She seems to be writing words with great wide loops, and she looks as though she is singing, moving her shoulders to some private melody.

I sniff, rub my knuckles across my cheeks.

He stands, goes into the bathroom and comes back with a tissue, tucks it into my hand.

"We'll start again," he says.

I CURL UP in the second chair, and he takes a pillow from the bed, props it behind me. "Better?"

I nod, refuse to feel ashamed. He's a stranger, anonymous, hired for my purposes. I don't need to explain, and he doesn't seem inclined to serve as avuncular comfort.

"Didn't you expect possible interference?"

I shake my head. "Not in a place like this."

"Why did you choose this hotel?"

I'm stung into defending my last stand. "You mean surely such a respectable place shouldn't have to deal with my body, doesn't deserve the hassle, the potential trouble?"

"No, but public places, even hotel rooms, are subject to interruption. Maids, bellhops, the screen of registration."

"Is it easier for you to do your business in somebody's home?"

"Actually, no. A hotel is much easier than a private residence. No snoopy neighbors, no barking dogs. It increases my anonymity, makes the job easier to walk away from. But that isn't necessarily simpler for you."

He is so calm. No wonder he's considered the best, the absolute artist of assassins. Every word he speaks or gesture he makes is attentive, focused, convincing. My other assassins should be here to take lessons.

"I thought this hotel would know what to do with a person who dies, accidentally or otherwise. The staff here are taught discretion, they materialize rooms when they're overbooked, they can bring breakfast at three in the afternoon, they'll know how to summon police and paramedics without causing a fuss. I'll be taken care of properly, protected from the oohs and aahs of gawkers or ambulance chasers. 'Oh look, a dead person. Is there blood? I want to see blood!' They probably have a system for removing a person, that shut-away marble staircase that floats up the middle wing."

Down that staircase they will take me, cocooned in a zippered body bag, the stretcher between the muscled arms of attendants bumping, the incline threatening to slide me off, me no longer, free, without muscle, an empty vessel.

Of course, they are far more likely to use the service elevator, its dented doors and bruised walls, to wheel a stretcher with my remains into that small room, thanking their stars that they don't have to hump me down a set of crooked stairs that wend and wend and wend five stories down.

But I prefer to think of myself as descending a staircase, the staircase turning secretly down the middle of the hotel, just a fire exit now, the doors forbidding entrance and lazy guests taking the elevators, preferring the slide and rise of machinery to the step of feet. I imagine the balustrades of the stairway, the rounded corners and turned newels, like a procession that I will pass, not I, but the dust I am.

⌒

"A BODY, NOT a person," says Derrick Atman dryly.

"Did I say person? A body, then."

"Decorum."

"Exactly. *Dulce et decorum est.*"

"Did you learn that in school?"

"I don't know. My education is limited, magpie phrases I've picked up between traveling and reading books."

"Did you go to school here then?"

"I finished Grade Twelve at Western Canada High, did well enough, I suppose, but not spectacularly, a seventy-two percent average, then went off to University of British Columbia for two years, more because of Vancouver than school. I took general courses, history, sociology, a B average, and then I couldn't take the frantic optimism of the West Coast anymore, packed up and came back here. It was the end of the boom, oil companies closing their doors every day, only the small scrappers left. Now the economy's starting to pick up again, you can hear that contented growl getting louder, expense accounts and golden Fridays will be back soon, more cautiously this time, but they'll be back."

"You would do well. Lots of courier work."

"Maybe, maybe not. Now, instead of using a courier, they can send their own executives on delivery trips, one of the perks of upper management. 'Here, take these assays to Jakarta.'"

"Jakarta?"

"Well, places like that."

"You sound cynical."

"Jakarta was a city I couldn't wait to leave. I could hardly breathe for the day and a half I was there."

"Too different from Canada?"

"Oh, I've eaten enough humble pie not to be a North American chauvinist. Do you know what was unbearable?"

"Tell me."

"The children, four- and five-year old children, selling colored water between the lines of traffic, holding up plastic bags of livid pink and blue water, their own faces hot and flushed, their arms too tiny to reach the windows of the moving cars that they ran beside. I was in a taxi, going downtown from the airport. Their eyes boomed with fever, desperation, those bobbing plastic baggies slung on a stick over their shoulders, and the water sloshing in those laughable cartoon colors. . . ."

I want to cry again, but to distract myself turn toward the window to see the woman across. Her yellow-lit frame is empty.

He reaches out his hand, rests it on the arm of the chair between us. He is still wearing his gloves, those neat, shapely suede gloves. He says nothing.

"What right do I have to be miserable?" I ask. "Such terrible hope."

MY PROLONGED AND pathological restlessness terrifies me.

I pretend not to be afraid; I pretend exhilaration when I am poised to depart, when my bags are at the top of the stairs and my mail has been forwarded. I tell myself lies in order to get away, I stretch schedules so that I will be absent longer.

I weep with loneliness before I leave. My dear one never says good-bye, but holds my head against his chest.

⟋◯

"ARE YOU MISERABLE then?"

"Why else would a person choose to die? Why else arrange a death?"

"Some people want to die at the zenith of their lives. They imagine they can never be happier, they want to stop at that peak."

I have to turn and look at him, but he's serious.

"They're wise," I say. "Most people believe that happiness is foolish enough to continue, even grow."

"And you?"

"Let's say that I am not intensely miserable, and not intensely happy."

"Not intensely anything?"

"No."

"So you want conclusion. No hope for a change in pitch?"

"No. No intensity in sight. And I do not intend to look forward to tolerable dawns."

⟋◯

I DON'T HAVE to tell him that I want refuge from the personal. I am afraid of my interior despairs and ecstasies doled out for inspection by the curious, the presumptive stare of those who practice varieties of distance but grab for the juice of intimacy with greedy fingers. I'm tired of eyes watching my face, I'm exhausted by outsiders trying to imagine my dreams, dictating my desires. This is a world that wants us to display every intimacy.

My dear one never clutches at me, never mines my heart for his own sustenance. He never uses the word *should*.

Should. Ought. Need.

HOPELESS, THE LONELINESS of hotel rooms, with their four-square beds, their dense and beveled windows, efficient desks, closet doors ajar as if leaving a crack of air for clothes ghosts hanging in that shadow.

This will be the last, the last hotel room. The last room.

THE DISTANCE BETWEEN me and my dear one is like a mounting pressure of blue, a page torn from a phone book. Together,
we ignore the purl of clocks and lamps until we are wrenched apart again, the air gone cold between us and our voices reduced to Canada International, the paltry chemical of a photograph.

My dear one can warm a hotel room miles away, can speak me into his heart. So why do I insist on leaving?

"And what about your family, those who will feel responsible for your—abdication?"

I think of Tante Katje rather than my dear one. She is my window, a frame I encounter every Sunday afternoon when I'm not traveling, the two of us pecking like sparrows at her thick coffee and spice cookies. She can only see me Sundays because she volunteers during the week for the abortion clinic, escorting women past storms of rant and abuse, the demonstrators' hail of stony words, into the clinic.

I was surprised when I found out. I thought of her as living on the edge of crumbling age, shrinking now that Uncle Piet had keeled over in the bakery, all that sugar and butter finally congealing around his heart. I thought she was preoccupied with whist or with classes at the Kerby Centre. So long since I lived in her house I hadn't charted her changes. Opening the mail every day. Rushing to the few phone calls she might get. Shopping for one. Oh, I knew she still drove, the big Buick long and stately for such a small woman. But when I found out that she, in her glossy mink and her well-polished boots, was escorting women past chanting pro-lifers, I couldn't believe my ears.

"Tante Katje. It could be dangerous."

She stirred her finger around in a box of assorted fancy cookies, looking for the chocolate mint wafer. "That's why I do it. Those poor women, having to get an abortion, but first having to push and shove their way past a bunch of shouting zealots."

I couldn't help laughing. "I mean dangerous for you."

"Oh, that's the point, *schattebout*. They don't dare to abuse me, I'm a sweet old lady."

She looked like a chipmunk presiding over gleaming

furniture and polished china, alert, inquisitive, too innocent to know the risks she took.

"But Tante Katje . . ." I protested.

"Do you think you're the only one who can have adventures? I may not be jumping off and on airplanes every day, but I had my share, and this work is important; all it takes from me is my arm."

This was the woman who had given me a room and a key, clean sheets and a regular allowance when my parents went back to Holland and I refused my first opportunity to travel. Maybe I guessed that travel would undo me, but I cried for months, threatened to run away or kill myself if they made me go. She explained to them that it was better if I stayed, that they didn't want to upset my balance. I had nine o'clock classes and baby-sitting on Wednesdays, and teenagers shouldn't be uprooted. She would look after me, make sure I was on track. The right track. I can hear her now, logical, soothing, so that my parents finally shrugged, gave up on me.

She had the sense to leave me alone, did not cling or give much advice, short of telling me how to avoid yeast infections and how to make Dutch vegetable soup. She offered me butter cookies and a Saturday night curfew, and she took me to her doctor for birth control pills.

That Sunday afternoon I looked at her and began to understand that every person harbors a secret life, a private space too complex to be imagined. "Tell me."

"Tell you what? During the war I fell pregnant and had an abortion. It was terrible, a botch, and as a result I could have no children. So I help these women. They should be safe." She stated huge events matter-of-factly.

I could only gape.

"How would I have a child in the war? There was no food; in the hunger winter we lived from beet tops."

"You never told me."

"Oh, your mother didn't approve. No sympathy, she thought it was the judgment of God."

"And you never—"

"What?" She dipped her cookie into her coffee.

"Clung to me, turned me into your . . . child, made me a substitute." I hesitated to say as much so bluntly, but I was overwhelmed with admiration for her defiance, her measured coolness in my life, how she would touch my sleeve when I left for school but never kiss me.

"You are your mother's child, not mine. Although I enjoyed having you about, the doors needed to be slammed. Piet and I were too quiet, too wrapped up in the bakery and each other."

How little I knew her then, she who had taken such pains to offer me rules without punishment, who had curbed her own desire to mother by letting me imagine myself motherless. How little I know her still, although I suspect that she will understand my dying, her catholic acceptance hardy as ever. No doubt she will cry secretly; we are intensely and comfortably fond of each other, but then she will go on, imperturbable.

"Yes," I say to my assassin. "My aunt. Tante Katje. She always likes to hear where I've been, what it was like."

"Your travels."

"Yes, she's an armchair traveler. She came here from Holland in 1957 and has refused to step onto a plane or a train or a boat ever since."

"She's never gone back for a visit?"

"Absolutely not. My parents came at the same time, but they hated Canada, stayed for ten years and then returned. I was in high school, didn't want to change my life all over again. It was the end of the sixties. I fought to stay, and she helped me, persuaded them that I'd be fine, they shouldn't force me, she'd look after me. And she did, she and Uncle Piet, until he died."

"She sounds like the kind of woman young people call feisty."

I chuckle. "Oh god, she hates that. 'I'm not feisty,' she says. 'Just alive.' This is the kind of thing she would do, you know. When she gets sick, she'll arrange her own death, she'll refuse all hospitals and drugs and drawn-out lingering farewells and just pull the curtain. Decisive. Perhaps I should leave her your contact."

"But you don't worry that your death will distress her?"

"It will, I know she'll mourn, she'll miss me. I don't want to be flip, but she's had plenty to grieve over, and she takes care of it as compactly as she lives."

"Aren't you underestimating her resistance to loss?"

"But I can't make that my focus. She's an old lady, she'll last until she's ninety-nine, she'll drive until they take her license away, she'll go to yoga twice a week, she'll make a story out of me, she's a survivor."

"And you're not."

"I don't want to be."

I REFUSE TO let guilt enter this room. Tante Katje will go on, she will endure.

I have no endurance. I have been defeated by details.

ACROSS THE E-WING, the woman has returned. She flits around the room, picking things up, moving the chair, lifting her flung coat from the bed, presumably to hang it. I stand at the window, openly watching, curious at the eloquence of her movements, the anticipation of her limbs.

"Look," I say to my assassin.

He rises and stands beside me, the two of us a cutout shape, almost the same height, twins.

"What do you think?" he asks gently.

"She's waiting for her lover."

"Is that why she's so restless?"

"Maybe. She might be excited, nervous, even anxious."

"She's certainly waiting."

"Impatient, I'd say."

He chuckles. "Strange how we conjecture a story on the basis of watching."

"She's beautiful," I say, thinking of her dancing.

"You can't see that from here."

"I can imagine it."

The wind swoops and the curtains next to us bell out. It smells of sage, something green in the back of the chinook's throat.

"The chinook is moving."

"Yes, it's been coming all day."

He turns and reaches out a hand, although he stops short of touching my arm. "Let's go out."

"Out?" I tense. I have entered this room with finality, decided to stay here. This will be my last room, I won't have to set foot on another street.

"Look, there's no time limit. We've got all night. Let's go

out for a walk and a nice dinner. You've made me curious. I'd like to hear about your travels."

"You're trying to make me change my mind."

"No, I can't do that. I'd just like to feel the wind, see a bit of the city, eat a good meal. Once our business is concluded, I can't linger or explore this place, I have to leave as quickly as possible."

He's too plausible, too convincing. Of course, I demanded a credible assassin with a good bedside manner and a sense of humor. I asked for a man neither too large nor too small, clean, nicely proportioned, a man who enjoys the company of women, a man flexible and imaginative. How did they arrive at the characteristics that embody that? He's good, I like him fine, but I'm suspicious.

"Is this part of your approach?"

"Not usually. Most people are sick or desperate."

"You won't try to dissuade me?"

"I swear. You're probably hungry. I wager you haven't eaten all day, too busy tying up your loose ends. I haven't either, except for that cup of coffee, and you're an interesting client."

We stand, looking across at the woman, who is now perched on the end of her bed with the television clicker in her hand. She swings one leg and seems to be following the action of some comedy as avidly as she was writing earlier. This woman, I think, would never hesitate, never feel afraid.

A meal, a walk. Where's the harm? He has signed a contract, made a paid promise. He won't stop me. I won't stop him.

"ONCE YOU GIVE me the signal to proceed," he says, "nothing you say or do will stop me."

A BUZZ OF happy warmth, that hum of a business hotel enjoying prosperity, permeates the lobby as we step out of the elevator. People are scattered on couches, waiting to meet dinner engagements, lilies spike floral displays, a piano shivers in the direction of the ballroom. This is the hour when people rush to movies and concerts, when the first martini before dinner tastes sharp and flavorful, when the dull crust of day recedes. I'm surprised at the lightness of my step, how privileged, escorted, I feel. I walk close to Derrick Atman, even venture to take his arm, lightly, below the elbow.

"Are you afraid I'll run away?"

"Oh no, you can't," I laugh. "You know, I once saw a horse ridden through this lobby. During Stampede of course. I was at the concierge's desk, waiting to pick up a set of long-range targets to courier to Denmark, and a cowboy on a horse high-stepped his way past the doorman, in through the side door, in front of reception, and right to the middle of the foyer. The poor horse could hardly keep his balance on the marble floor. He looked as if the stunt he was supposed to carry out would do him in. But he managed to stand there, brace-legged, glaring, as if to assert that he was a Calgary horse, and this was his place."

Derrick Atman laughs. "Right here?"

"Right there," and I point to a spot under the raindrop chandelier.

"This is a peculiar city."

"No worse than *fasching*, where men expect to have their ties cut in half by scissors-happy girls on the streets of Munich. At least the cause for celebration here is earthy rather than religious."

We cross the lobby, the bell captain nods politely and the doorman spins the revolving door. I feel like a character in a movie, part of a script, and I anticipate the narrative that will unfold.

On the steps we hesitate under the elaborate canopy, breathe deep the evening's electricity.

"Taxi?" The doorman is prompt.

"No, let's walk," I say.

He raises his top hat. "Have a nice evening then."

We dismount the horseman's steps, leave the ornate portico of the hotel, turn left and at the corner left again. The chinook is starting to accelerate, the wind a clump of tumbleweed combing playfully at my hair.

Silently, companionably, we walk, passing a few secretaries in running shoes, two teenagers leaning together, a slim man with the collar of his overcoat turned up. Above, a train crosses, shunting grain from one part of the prairies to another, working its echo. We walk beneath, the dense rumble drowning out both wind and our breathing, the labor of iron wheels on iron track grinding us smaller and smaller. Can a person be absorbed by sound, practice forgetfulness in its barrel embrace? Under the overpass we stop, the growling belly-deep, pushing us toward the ground. We raise our hands to our ears, bend from the waist beneath the pinion of vibration. Only when the cars are almost across, rattling more loosely, fading, do we straighten, pull ourselves into motion again.

The underpass sidewalk slants upward, and we climb, coming out from beneath the track to the slightly tawdry reach of First Street, the Bible House, Rideau Music, Cedar's Deli, the TransAlta building, the refurbished block of Manhattan Lofts, the IODE shop and at the end of the street, Maxwell Bates' St. Mary's, the cathedral outlined in stark rare form.

Walking together seems effortless; our bones carry our stride as if we were creatures in a forest, camouflaged. He gestures at the illuminated spire. "It's a stunning building, beautiful lines."

"I've never been inside. Raised as a Calvinist. Are you Catholic?"

"No. My family was Quaker."

"Quaker? That's odd, in Winnipeg."

"There are more Quakers about than people imagine. It's a quiet religion; we practice faith by keeping silent."

"Seems more sensible than the votives of conversion. I seem to meet religious scouts everywhere. Their eyes are closed in prayer while one hand picks your pocket."

"I'm shocked at your cynicism."

"Those who keep their eyes squeezed tightly shut don't have to take account of what their hands do."

"But that isn't confined to the faithful." He nods at the cathedral. "Shall we go inside?"

I look at him sidelong. "Are you enlisting some kind of spiritual assistance?"

"No, I'm interested in architecture."

And then, like children, we join gloved hands and run across the snow-melting street into the park and up to the heavy doors.

I've never come here, although my dear one has told me stories about being an altar boy, the requirements of such duties, the quirks of various priests, the theater of mass. He makes everything a story, every story a touch, every touch a reassurance. I did not know how lonely I was until he convinced me to lower my porcupine quills, open my fists. Let go.

But I cannot afford to think of him, my short happy life with a man of kindness, patient enough to scrub the handles of knives, to tuck the sheets tight at the bottom of the bed. Kindness is underrated, it should head the characteristics that women seeking lovers advertise for. Instead, they fall for money or looks, flashy cars, leather jackets.

We push inside, the hush of cool light and the faint smell of incense a quiet layer after the wind. The water in the font bears a faint sheen of oil, the tapers under the statue of Mary melt toward a dawn that I will not have to meet.

We tiptoe, speak in whispers, mass just over, the church settling toward night.

"You know, I've gone into cathedrals in so many cities, and yet I've never been inside this one. It's so—other worldly."

"Home is never a tourist site, is it?"

"No. And so we miss its secrets."

"People only explore their home cities with guests. I'm the same; never go to the parliament buildings or the Red River or the art gallery unless someone is visiting."

We sit on a stiff pew, wait for a requisite stillness, meditative space. I think of prayer, that I ought to unload my soul and, despite my agnostic heart, make some confession. After all, this is the night of my death. I will be crossing the barrier of human repentance. And cannot imagine what I should confess. Unhappiness? Plenty of that, yes. Desperation? Not really. Unkindness? Oddly, through all my uneven years, I think I was specifically unkind only when I refused to return to Holland with my parents. I haven't inflicted myself much on others. My greatest unkindness has been my refusal to connect, the safe distance that I wager from the world. What other sins? Greed? My possessions could hardly measure up to acquisitiveness. Sloth? Yes, some laziness, this act I intend to carry out is possibly born of laziness more than despair. I'm tired, I'd like to sleep.

Any other sins? Restlessness. A given. My restless heart, my restless travels, my restless bed, my restless contact lenses, my restless fingernail polish, my restless boots, my restless coffee grinder. Buses, taxis, airports, suitcase straps, lost earrings, forgotten raincoats, cheesy movies, smudged mirrors. Restless everything. Restless restlessness.

WE LEAVE THE cathedral and meander, turning west and south. We pass a funeral home, the shuttered building exuding an air of chill respectability.

"Have you made arrangements?" asks Derrick Atman.

"With a particular funeral parlor? Isn't that going a bit far?"

"Lots of people do. They want everything settled, from the hymns to the disposition of their bodies."

"I've asked to be cremated. Tante Katje shouldn't have to keep a grave clean."

"That's why?"

"I want to be erased, I want no corner of this world taken up with my square footage."

"Very environmental," he says dryly, and we both laugh.

We loiter, stopping to look at shops, people angled toward one another over the tables in pubs and restaurants. I give him my Calgary historical tour, tell him about the way downtown is cupped between the railroad track and the river, how the skyscrapers have grown into their own clump of Babel, how the belt line hovers just beyond downtown, how pockets of neighborhood emerge beyond this central cluster of light. We make a detour and I point out Nellie McClung's house, then the damelike façade of the Memorial Park Library.

"My first job was there, doing research in the Glenbow archives, searching for kernels of fact that could be distilled and sold."

"That sounds interesting."

"Yes, if I had been working for myself. But I was working for a difficult man, a historian of western politics. It looks like a dowager there, doesn't it?"

"The building."

"Yes. Odd place, breathing ghosts." I do not tell him that the historian was one of my first assassins, that I was working within a death scenario, although I didn't know it then. That was before I developed my impermeability, before I arrived at this turtle shell.

We turn west and north again so that we are headed back to the phalanx of buildings outlining the downtown core, admire the awkward grace of those glass towers, their infinite windows, their scanty eyebrows.

I gesture at the strange forest we are about to enter. "They're like glossy tombstones, aren't they? Beautiful, glistening tombstones."

～◯

WE CROSS UNDER the tracks at Fifth, the traffic headlights against us, emerge to the intersection at Ninth. Through the door of Cowboys gusts a riff of guitar, the chortle of chairs and glasses and persistent drinkers. "That's Calgary," I gesture.

"The assumed identity that becomes real. Be careful how you dress up."

"Is that like 'Be careful what you wish for'?"

"Similar. It's why the east won't take us seriously, because we dress up in cowboy clothes every Friday, like kids who've been given a set of cap guns. We're brash, delighted with our own ability to break rules, to wear blue jeans to work, to ride horses into hotels. We always bounce back from down times, blossom at the oddest moments. Calgary swings between the wild wind of a chinook like this and the solid heat of a late autumn day. If unreality is the hallmark of modern cities, then Calgary insists on hyper-reality, those glass canyons, the mirage of mountains, the awkward foothills."

"Is Calgary completely introspective?"

"Oh no, the opposite. It looks everywhere and fails to notice that its own shoelace is untied." I feel as if I have to laugh at my diatribe. "I'm lecturing."

He stops and steps in front of me, blocking my way. He bites his lip, then declares, as if it is a breach of contract for him to speak like this, "You love it here. You love this place."

I look away from him toward the lights that diffuse the melting snow. "Of course, I love it. Love is what makes us know how much we're doomed to fail. I want to leave because I love it. What am I to any city, any place, but a messenger girl, a cog who flies in and out, who goes home to the condo and parks her car in the garage with a grateful sigh that the wind and snow can't cover it, who sleeps a few restless nights, and then wakes to another hopeless morning, life an arrangement of shapes beyond the door."

"But we all have such lives, and yet they're important enough, they include fireworks and fishing and saskatoon pie. It's not easy to abandon saskatoon pie."

"Look," I say to him fiercely. I rest my clenched fists against the good wool overcoat buttoned up his chest. "Let me tell you, I am only one of many many women who wake in the middle of the night going over the tenuous knowledge they've uncovered, who count all the promises they've been made and who know there is nothing to be done with that wisdom, nothing at all."

"Do you believe that?"

"I believe it. I know it. Even better, I accept that fact. Most women learn it and then spend the rest of their lives trying to forget or ignore what they've learned. They get what they settle for, which makes their lives dreadful, imprisoned by pantyhose and casseroles and daycare and Valium. I refuse to settle for what I've been dealt. It's not enough."

He has caught my clenched fists in his gloved hands. Holding me there, he bends his head above mine for a moment, almost as if in prayer, then releases me and turns to walk again. Without a word. He will not stop me.

"AND SO YOU," he says quietly, the traffic passing us in waves of sound, "don't think it's worth trying to change anything."

"I would rather be sorry than safe. But that's not so bad. 'When I am dead, my dearest, Sing no sad songs for me. . . .'"

He spins around. "Is that it? You want to be remembered?"

I throw my arms wide, gesture at the sky. "I want to be forgotten."

"But you're fearful that you won't be?"

Perhaps I am afraid that no one will speak of me at all. My dear one. He would not help me. He promised that if I left, he would erase me.

I DO NOT tell Derrick Atman how I fight persistent home-sickness.

How the smell in other people's houses makes me catch my breath, how the splutter of frying hangs in a kitchen, the blue tang of mineral salts stirs a bathroom. Time emanates waiting, and history has a smell, powerfully musty, mute with long division.

But it all proceeds at a distance from me, the homeless one.

"SO YOU TRAVEL to escape yourself?"

I won't answer that question. "Oh," I say, "travel will come up with all kinds of temptations. Shall I stop over for a few days in London, see a play? Shall I try to find a baroque parador on the coast of Spain? Shall I let narrow streets distract me with their crossword? Shall I breathe the air of Mozart's many apartments and pretend that he is still a presence, effervescent, annoying?"

"And what do you answer yourself?"

"I want to stay home." I thought traveling would give me a perspective, a point of view, a character. Such a long and zigzagged search, and I managed to fail. I say this to my killer. "I failed."

"Failed?"

"I looked for a person I could be. I searched for—ha, how Canadian of me—an identity."

"Everyone wants to be a definable person. But clear edges, not blurred or torn or smudged, that's impossible."

"An apple is an apple. Some solid shape should be possible for a person. But it's not. So you are here."

"We are here," he says.

HERE. WE TURN at Stephen Avenue, wander past the castle of Bankers Hall, the elaborate web of plus-fifteens threaded overhead. On the street, people have opened their coats, walk more slowly, without the hunch of arms and the close hug of the body that signals cold.

We've turned ourselves inside out for the chinook's mirage. Me and my assassin, blown by wind.

A COUPLE OF blocks to the northwest, right around Sixth and Seventh, we can make out a high-rise that seems to reflect the shadow of a different building. Barely visible in the settling darkness, the outline of an imaginary building etched on the side of a building reminds the city that these are all illusory structures held up by hope or other acts of imagination, possibly nothing more than façades, elaborate gestures of architecture.

"There," I point it out to Derrick Atman. "A self-conscious building."

He stops, leans his head back. If I were a sculptor I would

create a statue in exactly that pose, an eloquent-bodied man in a proper overcoat leaning back, hands in his pockets, to observe the sweep of a skyscraper. A perfect gesture for Calgary, where the businessmen look straight ahead or at their feet, despite the glass mirrors flashing semaphore around them.

"Why self-conscious?"

"Well, like a woman looking into a compact, the building can't escape its own reflection."

"Okay, it's immodest, but still, there's an element of shyness there."

"You're a kind critic."

"It's your favorite building."

"It is," I admit. "It wears its own admission of defeat. During the day the glass is browny-pink, the shadow building almost sinister in its wrap-around hold on the bottom."

"Like the interior of a mind."

"Yes, buildings, like people, have character. That one reminds me of myself. Wearing its own projection."

"That's your choice."

"Maybe I have no choice."

HERE ON THE street, I can feel the unutterable answer my indiscreet heart seeks.

Language makes us restless. If I could rest in language, I might be less impatient, I might be able to mime contentment.

I should be content, willing to inhabit the silent space I share with my dear one. My dear one. We avoided saying the obvious. It's snowing. I'm tired. When are you done work? Can you pick up a loaf of bread? Now I think we should have used that language, used it to touch each other. Instead, we relied on physical touch, that short-lived eloquence.

And I'm shy, inarticulate, my misery dumb in its miming, and the only request I could make, one that he said no to.

⟋◎

"WHERE SHALL WE eat?"

Derrick Atman's question is almost domestic, the tone of a man asking his wife of many years what would please her.

I don't know this luxury, the habit of time. I've been with my dear one a mere two years, and then you could hardly call that long, since we've been apart more than we've been together. And now I'm about to keep it so.

⟋◎

WE'RE WALKING OPPOSITE The Bay now, its curved arcade sheltering display windows. I tug Derrick Atman across the street, stand with him under the portico. I love this store's resilience, the building as much a part of my long childhood as Tante Katje. I always did my Christmas shopping here, the atmosphere bustling and yet less ferociously mercantile than the malls.

"They look real," says Atman, gesturing at the statue of the two rotund businessmen.

"They are. Part of the city. There's a good little place along

First Street here. It used to be a shop, well, two shops really. A haberdashery, and next to it a sex shop."

He laughs. "Have they kept the inventory?"

"Oh no, they broke down the wall between the stores and it's a wine bar now, warm, good atmosphere. They usually have a decent Rioja by the glass. Bistro-type food. Shall we try it?"

We turn south again, on the street that will lead us back to the Palliser. I don't want to get too far away from my respite, I want to keep my assassination in sight.

The heavy door to Divino scrapes against the old wooden floor. Small round tables nest in the once–clothing store's side windows, the smell of ginger and garlic resonates. We wait to be shown to a seat, and again I tentatively elbow my relative comfort with Derrick Atman—that a man who will be death's accomplice is so easy to be with. But then, I described the characteristics that I wanted in detail, even down to the way this person would treat a pet or a child. The agency seems to have fulfilled my request with such exactness that I'm almost shocked. I nudge this thought curiously. Did I secretly want the assassin to fail, giving me an excuse to kill the contract?

The waitress puts us in the corner of what was the north display window so that we look onto the street. I can watch the hotel, which presides solemnly across Ninth, the five boulevard lights on either side of the entrance steps, spotlights shining up under the ornamental trees fronting the façade, lit as if to illustrate a Victorian tale. I ask him to sit in the corner so I am facing east, can see the whole sweep of building, the white sleeves over the windows, the brick solid as posterity.

When we've hung our coats and seated ourselves on the somewhat precarious chairs, Derrick Atman looks across at me and nods. "We've come full circle. We're right opposite the hotel."

"I know."

"Keeping your eye on me, are you?"

I bite my lip and nod. He's expensive enough that I know he's legitimate, but I've traveled for years to get to this moment. I'm afraid that this completion, this arrival, will slip away. I've come too far to turn back now.

～∽

THE WAITRESS BRINGS us menus and asks what we would like to drink, and I am saying, "Red wine," when I notice that Derrick Atman has taken off his gloves, those gloves that at first I found so sinister and now have grown accustomed to. His right hand is bandaged.

"Shall we have a bottle?" he asks. "Surely, yes. We have a right to relax."

"The Rioja is good," I say helplessly, repeating myself.

"Fine. Let's have that then."

Even as the waitress leaves, I have trouble pulling my eyes from his hands, beautiful hands, articulate and smoothly jointed just as I imagined, although they are clenched a little, and the right bandaged, gauze wrapped neatly around his palm.

He does it again, that gesture of turning his palms out, as if to show me that they contain no sinister secret.

"Have you hurt yourself?" I ask lamely, imagining knife slashes, terrible burns, maybe even an indelible stain of blood.

He looks down at the hands that he has lain, as if they are separate from him, palms up on the table between us. "I suffer from Dupuytren's contracture. It's a condition where your fingers curl into a permanent bend because the tissues thicken

86

and shorten, tethering the tendons. The result is that a hard lump forms on the palm of the hand, and it spreads to form a band of pressure under the skin until you can't straighten your fingers. I've just had surgery on the right hand. They cut and separate those bands of thickened tissue to free the tendons and to restore flexibility. I'll have the left one done in a couple of months."

I cannot help myself, reach across and touch with my fingertips, an uncertain tenderness, the wounded hand that has promised to release me. "Does it hurt?"

"It did. It's much better now, but my hands get cold easily, so I tend to wear gloves all the time, unless I'm eating or doing something that requires finger work."

So he will not use his hands to kill me, does not intend to throttle me, a closure which requires strength, unremitting pressure.

He smiles. "No, I won't be using my hands to commit any violent act."

I blush. "I'm sorry, I—"

"Of course. It's uppermost in your mind. I understand."

"How did it happen?"

"The condition may be inherited or caused by clenching your hands around vibrating equipment, but I haven't done much of that in my life."

Genetics is a cave, a hollowed out spoon within the earth that holds the potential for hurt.

"Do you think people inherit sadness?" I ask.

"They say that depression is passed on. But does the origin or cause matter? Isn't how people cope with what they carry more important?"

"'Palm trees don't grow on ice. 'A quote I've never forgotten, Umberto Veruda, I think. That might be an epitaph for the genetics of sadness."

"But doesn't ice have its own life? Its own beauty? Its own crystalline growth?"

"Only if you are an aficionado of cold, and I am not quite capable of imagining green fronds where there is only hoarfrost."

"But hoarfrost is beautiful!"

"To optimists and over-romantic poets."

He looks out the window, down the hurrying street. "Have you—?" His flesh seems to hesitate, pull inward, then straighten with courage. "Have you thought of getting fixed up with one of these new drugs—Prozac or—?"

I snort with laughter. "Are you trying to make yourself unemployed? Or better yet, you could be a pharmaceutical representative. The scourge of doctors, hitting clinic after clinic with free samples."

His face is inscrutable. "I'm serious."

"Do you think some chemical concoction can erase grief? And should I want it to? Why not be sad, why not be willing to quit the world? Too many people hang on when they should give up. They are convinced that they ought to be satisfied with the occasional spicy taco, a box of truffles on special occasions, holding the channel changer in one hand, driving the minivan ten kilometers over the speed limit. What an empty set of motivations, a mockery. Most people haven't the imagination to get themselves murdered."

"But ordinary things are comforting. People make do."

"Why? Why should they? And even if they will, why should I? Making do is not enough."

HE TOUCHES MY hand lightly. "Let's forget our work and eat something delicious."

Under the small table our knees bump together. The menu is a large cardboard sheet promising everything from eggplant to cranberry duckling, and I feel suddenly ravenous. He's right, I spent all day clearing up details so that Tante Katje will not face questions or accusations or banks or insurance companies. And I spent most of last night writing my dear one a letter, a letter I know is woefully limited, filled with my terrible silence, my cowardly decampment. Before I checked in, I dropped it through the mail slot of the main postal depot, so it will be sorted tomorrow morning, delivered to him in a day or two. I've been fainthearted about not telling him. Although I did ask him to help me, and he refused.

We order eggplant dip to start and settle back into the hum of voices, the warm flicker of candles. I'm able to watch the Palliser, kitty-corner in my line of vision and then realize that from here I can see the woman's room. Her window, at the corner of the fifth floor, on the farthest east wing of the E, faces west. Mine, directly opposite, faces east. And squinting, I can make her out, still there, walking up and down as if pondering a question or a problem that must be solved.

"Look," I point.

He half-turns, sees immediately that I've resumed my watch, and chuckles. "Must be your guardian angel."

"Hardly. I don't merit one."

He peers at the woman's pacing. "She's worse than you are. So, are you restless because you travel, or do you travel because you're restless?"

I don't answer immediately, watch the step and halt, step

and halt of her shape as she crosses in front of the uncur-tained window. "She's waiting for something that matters," I murmur.

"We're all doing that."

I have to look at him again, but cannot meet his eyes, which are watching his own bandaged hand touching the stem of his wineglass.

⌒⌒

"OKAY, I ADMIT as much," I say. "I've been using distance to meddle with the plot of my life, to alter my course, to escape, plunge headlong into a denial that I have always known I should confront. There, I've confessed."

"What have you been denying?" Derrick Atman asks.

"My own disaffection, my inability to deal with mundane cruelties. I want to destroy the day-to-day abrasions of life's oblivious plot. I can no longer swallow guidebook advice. Here is your street, here is your work, here are the people you must nod and smile at, whose only goal is to make others trip and fall, whose only desire is to set the innocent on fire."

"No one disregards cruelty or poison."

"Oh, but we do. We cancel our disgust, contain our pain, or we die. And so I've been trying to erase my sensitivities through insistent movement, leaving I'm Away, Do Not Disturb, hanging on my doorknob, my friends having to be patient as those old-time photos, where the clothes pretend you are historical.

He looks quizzical. "So you're running away."

"No, that's too simple. I'm using travel to erase everything else, to escape the unbearable, to believe myself invisible."

"You want to be invisible?"

"Of course, even if it's impossible. Every country I travel to proves me visible—my clothes are wrong, my accent is wrong, the very cut of my hair is asymmetrical, out of culture. Even if I never open my mouth, my shoulders and wrists betray me, and the flash in a stranger's eyes that says *foreigner, vreemde* is worst of all. So I try countries where I'm really visible, my skin whey compared to everyone else. I juggle my visibility even though I want to blend into the wallpaper as if I were the hidden wall underneath."

"Like that building, visible and invisible playing together, reflecting a reflection that isn't there."

"Maybe."

"Like contact lenses?"

"No, more like shoes. North Americans will always wear runners or gym shoes, declare their allegiance to Nike or Brooks without blushing. Europeans wear discreet leather walking shoes that can pass for dress shoes. The rest of the world wears what is comfortable or what they are used to or what they damn well please. You see, the ability of feet to change, say, into a pair of high-heeled pumps for an evening at the opera, that's a signal. Feet demand familiar shoes, rubbed straps and shoelaces that have settled into their eyelets. You see? You see?"

"I don't. But it's a good confession."

⁓

THE WOMAN'S NOT afraid of visibility. She hasn't bothered to pull her curtains, hasn't troubled herself with voyeurs. She's living her own life, unafraid of choices, even though she's waiting. Or at least that is what I imagine, seeing her framed there in the window, visible but oblivious.

⟡

HE FOLLOWS MY eyes but doesn't turn to look. "You're watching her."

"That's what I learned to do as a traveler. Watch. Now I'm suspicious of my own movement. I suspect that the physical act of displacement we call traveling is my voyeurism seeking to reach some pinnacle of experience, a gourmet acquisition of strangeness through dislocation, with all relevant assumptions about what is capturable. Mmm, this eggplant dip is wonderful."

He throws back his head and laughs. "Whew!"

"Oh, I can go on about how that uneasy zenith becomes nadir in the mirror-based contortions that the traveler engages between self and other, familiar and strange, anticipation and surprise, making for a climate of self-congratulation that does not recognize its own temperate zone. There is nothing sub-zero or tropical about the contemporary experience of travel — climate-controlled hotels, restaurants, theaters, tour buses, museums, even, damn it all, ski hills and skating ovals."

He is still chuckling. "You certainly aren't climate-controlled. I was under the impression that you think of yourself as a kind of delivery slave, and then you start spouting this philosophy."

"Oh, I am a delivery slave. But I'm a picara too, traveling for the sheer hunger of movement, traveling in order to escape my essential laziness. The picaresque tradition historically argues for travel as a self-conscious activity, metadestinational, wickedly aware that it seeks its own extinction. Picaresque travelers long to behave badly, and while they see themselves as unmaskers of a hypocritical world, they also know themselves to be cowards with a failed cause, able only to pursue their own pursuit. So I work to stay ambiguous, watching myself following myself and rejoicing in the small indiscretions I manage to commit."

"Are you a traveling troublemaker then?"

"No, unfortunately not. The art of travel, its passion, is passé, which reduces travel to tourism, a destinational itinerary, an achievement list of geographies."

"Places on a trophy shelf?"

"Exactly. So, I travel for my work, but I know I'm an outsider, a failed participant, repentant rouge, mere tourist. Nevertheless, like most twentieth-century denizens with the means and the excuse, I revel in my touristry, as if it will reward me with insights that I can barter for a few square inches of sitting on the edge of Nose Hill with the grassy wind blowing in my ear."

"But you know the lie of your experience. You've diagnosed it yourself."

"Oh sure, I know my limitations, I recognize the sham of a suitcase and a passport. That's why you're here. I want to make it clear to myself that I haven't totally, irrevocably, succumbed to fakery. Just one honest gesture, that's all I want."

❧

"I SUSPECT," HE says softly, biting a triangle of foccacia, "that you think too much. Why not live in the moment, enjoy the air or the food or the museums wherever you go, and leave it at that?"

The woman is still pacing, running her fingers through her hair, which I have decided is shoulder length, rumpled, although I can't possibly see such details from this distance.

"Somehow, I can't escape my own sense of fraudulence. I don't belong wherever I am, and I don't belong here."

"Perhaps you should have returned to Holland with your parents."

"Perhaps. My life would have been different."

"Do you see them?"

"Oh, I visit if I get anywhere near Rotterdam. But we're separated, their lives went off in another direction. They remember me as a child, and they can't reconcile the adult I've grown into with the child that they've fixed in time."

"All parents do that to a greater or lesser extent. I catch myself doing it with my kids. Remembering a particular afternoon when we went skating and then being brought up short to see them, adult, serious, unable to remember skating together at all."

I take a sip of wine, glance again at the woman, who has crossed her arms over her chest, who appears to be inventing a strategy while she paces, stopping, then taking another step.

"Do you think," and my voice feels hollow, "people should be stamped by experience, say a physical mark, like being pierced by an arrow, so that a person carried visible evidence showing that they'd actually visited—and been scarred by—a particular place? Tattoos, stigmata maybe, to inscribe a certain moment."

"Documentation fever. I hate the idea. More and more, everything we've done must be proven with a diploma, a confession, a résumé, a passport stamp, a registry signed and dated. As if the world is a version of court, as if private knowledge should be outlawed."

"You believe in privacy then?"

"Absolutely. That's why I do this work. And so do you, or you would never have hired me. One of your stipulations is the absolute privacy of the choice you've made."

"To be killed."

"Exactly."

"But it still seems planned, documented. It would be better if it were accidental."

"Arranged accidents are no longer accidental. And death is an inescapable registry."

I cannot stop myself from watching that restless woman. "Do you think her life is arranged or more accidental?"

He chuckles and turns to glance at the hotel window. "Right now I'd say that some arrangement has been accidentally disarranged. She seems awfully impatient, as if she's been waiting too long at someone else's mercy and can't do what she wants."

"But she seems completely at home there."

"In a strange place, we turn to what is familiar, don't we?"

"That's for sure. I always felt caught in a conspiracy of surveillance and collation, carefully controlled strangeness pandering to what I recognized. There's something awry there. Travel is supposed embrace what's different, so why do we end up clinging to what is familiar, or worse, commonplace? Nothing surprises, just reaffirms."

"And you believe that you should get what the tourist pamphlet promises."

"Why not? Something to make me understand why I'm bereft, isolated, yet connected to rituals and gestures I've never encountered. I got so frustrated I used to welcome physical pain, pounding head, aching shoulders, angry joints, jet lag, indigestion. If I felt pain, I thought, it might be possible to register difference."

"Do you take photographs when you travel?"

"Oh never. I won't carry a camera."

"You're afraid of cameras?"

"I am not afraid of cameras—no, the truth is I'm terrified of the technical arrogance of good cameras, their lenses and aperture speeds and light meters and their snub black smugness. I've learned to be wary of the click—have you noticed that now it's sinisterly inaudible?—that pretends to capture a moment. What's the effect of pushing a mechanical button to record a person smiling in front of some historic façade? It seems to show that the person in the photograph wants to prove something, make an immaterial experience visible."

"Traveling without a camera is an unforgivable sin. In all those trips, did you never take pictures? You could have used them, become a travel writer or a photographer."

"No, I can't bear to take pictures, can't bear to have pictures taken of me."

"Why not?"

"Photographs are lies. They wait for misperception and spring on it."

"They're a record of sorts."

"Shall I take a picture of you then and leave it on the night table for the authorities to find?"

"I think it wiser not to."

"There you are. Although any equivalence between pictures and real people is doubtful. People who believe in the ability of a photograph to identify someone are utterly gullible."

"You must have some pictures of yourself when you were a child."

"Meaning? Those pictures should comfort me?"

"Well, give you a sense of how you grew, perhaps a happier time."

"In every picture of myself that I have seen, and I've kept none of them, I was either in tears or on the verge of tears. In a few of them I was just past tears, and the manic smile that I put on for the camera is terrible to see. I have little wish to enlarge the record of that melancholy printed into negative and shadow, and ignored by everyone who thumbed those snapshots, even though it was so visible."

"And so you avoid cameras."

"I abhor them, their elementary authority, the way they can be punitive or misleading, the manipulative photographer's compositions."

"And so year after year, trip after trip, through countries that other people dream of seeing, you simply averted your eyes."

"No, I looked straight at everything without the intervention of a lens. I won't apologize for that. You know, I once saw the camera fiend to slay all camera fiends. I was on a boat ride through the canals of Amsterdam, a tourist trip, but oddly beautiful and one that I take every time I go there. We seldom get to see the shoulders and flanks of cities, everything is façade, the public face. Taking a boat ride through the canals is way of seeing how shipping and movement took place in the seventeenth century, the aspect of the houses from the water. Anyway, beside me was a woman who took, in less than two hours, eight rolls of thirty-six exposure film. She clicked and clicked, never took her eye from the viewfinder. I looked at the slime-green canals and the gabled houses with their hoist cranes, the elliptical streets converging and converging toward the city's sheltering dike, and I imagined how for her they were divided into a sequence of rectangular frames. All she'll remember is what she saw through her lens with that ferocious red light blinking in the lower right-hand corner."

"How long was the trip?"

"About an hour and a half. I watched her, fascinated, waiting to catch just one moment when she'd look directly at a door or a window, when she would face the world scrolling past. She kept on snapping, the mechanism whirring, except when she had to change film, and then she resolutely bent her head over the camera's intestines. She was expert at changing film in less than half a minute. When the boat docked at the end of the journey, she asked me if I could direct her to the nearest Taco Bell, which, in a city as replete with food as Amsterdam is, actually had the effect of striking me dumb."

"And so you have chosen never to record your journeys."

"I think the photographer has to take pleasure in the person or the landscape that she wants to capture. But when I take pleasure in a place, I don't want to interrupt by stopping to take a picture. And if I'm not experiencing pleasure, why bother with a camera?"

"You don't even want to remember a beautiful building?

"Me standing in front of the Arc de Triomphe, me with the Eiffel Tower in the background? I want to be unphotographable. I prefer the tyranny of my eyes and ears, my nose and fingers."

"And what if I took a picture of you now? As evidence that we've met."

"Dangerous for you, and it wouldn't turn out. I'm too far into that gray aura between those who are in the physical world and those who are ready to leave it. If I aimed a camera at myself in a mirror, the mirror would have no reflection."

He shakes his head. "Don't be romantic. So only spies and those who document atrocities should use cameras?"

"Yes, in the hands of the ordinary person, they are an affront. Who was it said, 'Tourists are terrorists with cameras, while terrorists are tourists with guns'? They both shoot what they can't tame."

"But you can't help looking at what you see. Does it matter if you take a picture?"

"I think you can't replace what your hand feels when you reach out and touch the roughened skin of a sun-warmed brick wall, you can't photograph the taste of barbecued Jamaica jerk chicken. But you remember them, you don't need a photograph to jog your sensory intelligence. Why are our eyes the only organ we don't trust? Why do we need stacks of photo albums?"

"But don't you forget?"

"Of course I forget. I suppose now, if I could search through shoe boxes and find a photograph of myself standing in front of the Great Pyramid in the strange light cast between those hewn blocks and the Egyptian sand, I'd be delighted at the effect of remembering my pose. But why? Because I want to remember the Great Pyramid? Because I want to reassure myself that I actually stood next to it? Because I need to know how tall I am in relation to it? Or because I simply want to have it, keep it, own it, take it away with me?"

"It would jog your memory."

"I think the desire to keep photographs is suspect. Why is a visual record so important? Do I need to remind myself, or does the photograph encapsulate a time and place that should be remembered imperfectly?"

"Stubborn amnesia."

"I want my memory to work without props, so that what's left is what I do remember. The camera censors what I'm convinced I have seen or touched. Whatever I experience that is different gets turned into its photographic record, almost a lie." I gesture toward the square of light that I have come to regard as the woman's frame. "How would you photograph her?"

"We're too far."

"No. A telephoto could do it."

"You mean to capture her as we see her?"

"I mean to capture her in any meaningful way. No quick photo can translate what we've watched and speculated and imagined about her."

"You could film her."

"Sure, but that would be limited by the window. We only catch glimpses of her when she passes in front of it."

The waitress appears, pours another glass of wine and takes away the empty eggplant dip plate. I realize I've been eating and talking, completely oblivious, my immediate goal forgotten.

"I'm sorry," I say abruptly. "I'm raving."

He chuckles. "You're surprising," he says softly, and reaches his bandaged hand across to touch my elbow. "You're alive."

REFUSING TO TRAVEL with a camera enables me to believe that I am traveling not only by suitcase and guidebook, but erratically, willing to take on the imprimatur of whatever chooses to single me out and mark me.

I thought I could become a version of notebook, blank pages loose and ruffled, a bill here, a leaflet, a scrap of ticket with the single word *wait* scrawled on its back. Of course, I deceive myself by even believing I am worthy of notice.

The planned trip, metaphored by photographs, is a setup, a tawdry gamble, like the columned ads in the Sunday paper placed by single white females looking for prospective mates. To lose expectation in both travel and its record is to live an unfinished cartography, following the street that never appears on the map, the name that vanishes once it has been spoken, the country that has never been visited.

I do not tell Derrick Atman, but I've kept one picture of myself framed on my dresser at home. I am standing beside the China Sea, posed on an old stone wall beside one of my assassins, a man whose name I have forgotten. I wear the yellow hand-painted pants that I later forgot in the hotel room, their side seams zippered and painted with stars, like children's parachute clothes. We are both looking away, as if hesitating in front of the camera, as if shy. I do not know who took the photograph or how it came to me.

The Straits of Malacca behind me shiver with light, reminding me of delicious dying.

I kept the photograph because he was the last assassin before I found my dear one.

⌒◡

"BUT," DERRICK ATMAN says suddenly, leaning toward me, "windows have stories too."

It's true. When I wake, I turn my face toward the dim square of morning light, wondering where I am. The mist drifts through that window, propped open with one of my boots, mist that might be Amsterdam's or Edinburgh's, or even the haze rising from the Arizona desert, where it is too dry to be misty.

Those windows repeat themselves all summer, all winter, poignant and confined. When I peer through them, I seem to glimpse a shiver of water far and far away, a touch of sea shimmering faintly under a cloud-moving sky. A dazzle of distance.

WHAT DOES SHE see, looking out her window? Can she make us out, two figures sitting in a dusky candlelit restaurant, talking about her? Is her impatience for herself or someone else? Does she expect immunity, or is she practical, goal-driven, ready to make a deal and file an agreement, then go on?

"Do you think windows have taught us to crave photographic moments?"

"No, it's the story behind the window, what we wish we could see. Like her." He gestures toward the building. "We want to know her story, but her window is a story itself."

I glance up just in time to see her kill the light. "She's gone out."

"Ah, exactly on cue! Here's our dinner. Now you'll have to stop watching."

"No, now I have to watch the door to see if I can catch her coming out of the hotel!"

He throws back his head and laughs. "You are entirely too curious to be ready to die."

"No, I'm not. Just because I watch her for a while doesn't mean that I intend to keep on watching."

He picks up his fork, his knife, gestures for me to begin eating. "You're hungry," he says.

And he's right. I'm famished.

"OKAY," I SAY, taking another sip of wine. I'm having a steak, something I haven't eaten for years, but this is my last supper, and steak is good in Calgary. It's wonderful, tender and rich and eloquently animal with a side of garlic mashed potatoes and roasted vegetables. "I'm interested in her restlessness because it reminds me of my own. And I'm restless because when I get home the only things I remember about the place where I've just been are mixed-up details arguing with one another. A fragment of garden, the knee of a statue, a door-knob. The only thing I can do is leave again, flee to another place."

"So you don't dare to stay home."

"It's perverse, isn't it? If I stayed home, I'd be a better person. Instead, I'm always fluttering off. And then I'm homesick."

"But once you get back here, you're dissatisfied."

"Oh completely. I can't wait to leave again. I want to run away from my friends, my house, Tante Katje, my lover."

"Your lover."

I swallow. My dear one's face, hard with love, stares into my eyes. "I want to vanish. I try to commit suicide. I fail."

"Your lover." Derrick Atman isn't going to let me escape, he refuses to drop the slip I've just made.

Carefully, I put my knife and fork down. "It's not relevant."

"Have you left him? Is it a him?"

"Would it be different if it were a woman?"

"No. Has he left you?"

"No."

Derrick Atman waits, an implacable edge to his stillness. He's too sensitive. I should have settled for a less aware assassin, one who would do the job fast, even crudely. But all the others were oblivious, and I hate oblivion so much.

"There's nothing wrong between us. That's not why."

"You haven't quarreled?"

"No, not at all."

"Not at all."
"No."

‧

EXCEPT THAT I wanted him to kill me. And unlike all the other assassins, he refused.

‧

I'M BLINDED BY tears again. Twice in one day, I've turned on the taps.

I blink, try to focus on the street beyond our table, and there she is, I'm certain, the woman in the window, striding as purposefully as if she hadn't been pacing her room, waiting. She's wearing a leather coat, high boots, her hair looks auburn, tousled, sexy. She walks as if the wind is part of her body, as if she breathes cinnamon brandy.

"Don't turn around," I say. "No, do. Look, there she is!"

He twists in his seat, watches the woman float down the sidewalk across the street, her quick energy displacing the air around her, her chin forward, hands thrust deep in her pockets. We both watch, crane our necks until she turns the corner at Eighth and is gone.

"She's even better than I imagined!"

"In a minute you're going to suggest that we follow her." He takes his napkin from his lap, grins. "Do you want to?"

For a second I'm tempted, and then I think, no, he's trying to distract me. Following her will displace the whole night, we'll never get to the crux of things. I shake my head. "It's just good to see her, to see her walking. She knows what she wants."

"Apparently," he says, "so do you."

⁓

"So, TELL ME more about your work," he says, picking up his fork again. "How do you arrange this jet-setting?"

"It's simple. The telephone rings, I lift the receiver, someone wants a patented type of canola seed delivered to the World Agriculture Association in the Hague. I get on the telephone, I have a gold card, I travel enough to have access to a special reservations line. In half an hour I've arranged another trip to Amsterdam, via London maybe, on a flight that will diagonalize the pole and tear down on the runways of Heathrow, where the double-decker buses go in circles and police dogs snarl around the baggage destined for Teheran. You see, it sounds so exotic, but it gets terribly commonplace."

"Except that if you're going to the Hague, you'll see your parents."

I nod. "If there's time, yes. I'll take them a jug of maple syrup and a box of smoked salmon, I'll stay for a night and eat too many almond cakes, and then I'll get back to Schiphol and fly home again."

"You make it sound like going to the grocery store."

"Except that, to me, grocery stores are more unusual. I miss daily shopping so much that I search out markets, crates of picturesque limes, piles of pears ripening into splendid curves. Naked food, flowers bunched in buckets, the awnings of venders hopeful against rain or wind. And I notice the differences, how the market in Trier is civilized with ripe cherries and mounds of vegetables, but in London the markets are flyblown, imitative, the food slightly past its prime. London venders would rather own an Oddbins Store and lounge behind a counter inside, while customers search out a smooth red for dinner."

"And your homesickness for shopping is why you want to stop now? To quit."

"Yes, I want to unpack that suitcase and kick it into the bottom of the closet. I don't want to gather together my meager clothes, my sad toiletry bag. I'm sick to death of folding my shabby raincoat over my arm, stepping out the door pretending to be purposeful. I want to stay put."

"Stay at home with this lover that you haven't quarreled with."

"That's not fair. And it's not your business."

"No, you're probably right." He raises the bottle. "More?"

I hold out my glass. I can even afford to get drunk tonight.

TRAVELING, I BECAME an antitravel ghost, an aubergine bruised without falling, a thin curtain sweeping aside rain. I was full of travel's ambiguous desires, but I was always unfulfilled, always frustrated.

The better to know I was not at home.

"And do you send postcards to your lover? Oh, I shouldn't say that. To other people?"

I ignore his suggestion, my dear one behind his query. "Sometimes. I tend to buy in bulk, you know, pick up six postcards of the Three Graces in the Edinburgh Art Gallery. I know I won't write them, and if I do, I won't manage to send them, despite the frequency of post offices or the concierge's express desire to mail them on my behalf, even if I have the correct stamps neatly arranged in a pocket of my wallet. I end up taking the postcards home, adding them to the drawerful in my kitchen."

"So you save them?"

"If I send postcards, I send them from home, and write them pretending that I'm still away. It's postcard fraud."

"Have you tried other jobs?"

"Ha. Not really. Although for a time I worked in a kiosk on the Leidseplein in Amsterdam, exchanging currencies."

"What was that like?"

"Changing every kind of money into guilders? Pretty dull. I was trying to reconcile with my parents, and because I was born there, I was allowed to work in Holland. Funny, people always laughed at the small dime, the *dubbeltje*, you know. It looks like a toy dime, almost invisible. Everyone had the same reaction. 'Oh, what a sweet coin.'"

"As if coinage were sweet."

"Exactly. But it was a job until I was robbed."

"How?"

"A desperate druggie. There's a button next to your knee, you're supposed to push it the minute you're nervous, but the police are slow, they take their time, and I was actually frightened—he held a knife over my wrist, and I thought that I would lose my hand to him."

"Which one?"

"The left. His hand was shaking so hard, I thought he was going to slip, and the knife was rusty, god."

Atman reaches out, turns my hand over. "No scars."

"No, he didn't even nick me. I gave him the money. We weren't supposed to do that, we were supposed to hold out, make them talk, tell them that we didn't have access to large amounts. I didn't care. I wanted my hand back."

"So he reached in and grabbed your hand?"

"It's hard to do, there's a closed glass circle, but he turned it and caught me."

"I thought those money changing booths were totally inaccessible."

I look at him. "Maybe I wanted to give it to him. Maybe I wanted an assassin. Maybe I just wanted to lose my job."

How MUCH DO I dare to claim? Can I sigh and repeat James Joyce's lament, "And trieste, ah trieste ate my liver"?

Such brilliant disembowelments have never happened to me. My assassins, alas, were all petty thieves.

I DID MEET up with an assassin in Trieste. He was clumsy, almost drove the car over the edge of a low concrete ledge. All the streets are built up the hill of the town, and those ledges mark the grade. Only the cries of some archetypal women swathed in black clothes made me tell him to stop, and there we were, inches from an accident, but an accident too small to accomplish more than inconvenience, not even minor bloodshed.

That was when I understood I couldn't rely on driving, when I started using trains or buses, the measure of my own feet.

Trieste crouched low in the summer heat and waited for us to make mistakes. The cafés around the Canal Grande were tawdry, and that particular assassin refused to enter the more palatable restaurants. He was afraid of tablecloths. Too expensive, he said. I have always been too expensive, a costly woman. Tante Katje encouraged me, told me to ask for the best, never to settle for goldfill or plastic flowers.

My dear one laughs at my love of fresh flowers, how I want their leaves patterning my table, petals dropping softly as they loosen.

I crossed Trieste alone, the cats that thronged the Scala Santa feral and snarling, the children running from their nursemaids, and me, adrift without a word of Italian and completely bereft, desperate to be erased. Trieste is sleepy, unimportant, passed over by its odd positioning. Trieste was where I was first murdered, where the hands around my throat tightened until I could not breathe.

In Trieste I began to understand that words can slice a heart to ribbons. The cold Adriatic lapped against my hazy inarticulate pain.

It was there I grew restless, started looking for a city of my own, Calgary too far away, its azure mountains too pristine, crabapples hanging from the trees like lamps, red and tense with tart, waiting to fall to the ground. Waiting to rot.

After all, who comes from Calgary? Who lives in such an impossible city, brash, arrogant, indelibly new? Only a few misbegotten cowboys and singers. Oil executives and escape artists.

I intended to write a fan letter to Jann Arden, the pure groan of her singing body coursing the thread of earphones I carry to remind me of home. Too late, that's one thing I left undone today. She'll never know how much I listened to *Happy?* I wanted to buy her fresh flowers. To thank her, let her hear me listening.

⌒○

WHEN THE WIND blows the leaves away from the trees, I sit by my window and weep. There is no such thing as the sadness of angels. My dear one loves me too much. He refused to kill me.

⌒○

"OH YES," I say to Derrick Atman, "of course cities have personalities. They're like people we live with, try to understand, fight, hold in our arms. People we miss desperately and then take for granted."

"So which is your favorite?"

"In the whole world?"

"In the whole world."

"That's impossible to answer. Every place has its own nose and ears, its own walk, its own elbow style."

"Well, which city intrigues you most?"

"That's easier. Europeans accept shabbiness that North American eyes can never adjust to. I like macabre places. Vienna."

"Vienna?"

"Yes. Have you ever been there?"

He slides his knife and fork neatly across his plate. "I have been to Winnipeg, Ottawa, Halifax, Honolulu, Vancouver, Philadelphia, Mexico City, and now Calgary. That's it."

"You've never been to Toronto?"

"No."

"Come on."

"No. Toronto's never come up. Maybe—what did you say before?—no one there has the imagination to get killed."

"AND YOU'VE NEVER been to Europe?"

"No, never. So tell me about Vienna."

"Well, you can forget the Vienna Boys' Choir and the famous Sachertorte. You can forget Mozart and the Lippizaner stallions. They're all tourist shows. The real city shudders under the weight of what they call its disastrous imperial past, suffocates behind leaden frames mixing Baroque, post-Gothic, Renaissance. At the turn of every corner, you see a façade, sometimes imposing, sometimes . . . well, innocent. Look ahead on a narrow street and some heavily sculptured portal looms, look over your shoulder and another frowns behind."

"So it's full of old buildings."

"Yes, like strange faces. There's one building that the Emperor Frans-Josef even complained of, said that it had no eyebrows. It's still there, although the empire is long gone."

"The empire?"

"The Austro-Hungarian Empire. The one that committed suicide right after the First World War. It's a covetous old city. Everywhere amidst that polished brass past, you see the tension of rank and privilege and the overprotective assurance of what was the Holy Roman Empire."

"The Holy Roman Empire?"

"The Austro-Hungarian Empire. Neither holy nor Roman, but they needed the blessing of the church."

"So why is it so intriguing?"

"Well, it's full of death. Underneath the waltzes and *Sachertorte* is a whole spectrum of gloriously elaborate death. Viennese streets cherish their lugubriousness, all winding alleys or eccentric passages, unhappy, prone to early cul de sac. And everything that's been pulled down or buried has as much weight as what's left, present and alive. You can hardly breathe for the scent of death, the wonderful groan of| continual mourning. That's why the eyelids of the glazed windows seem human, why the façades of the various *palais* seem like faces."

"Even the buildings are human?"

"Almost. Of course, Vienna is a cliché, seduced by its own intricacy, caught in the spell of post-Gothic imaginations. Viennese streets gleam with the polish of a historical city gone tourist, a place reduced to a Disney excursion."

"It's completely tarted up?"

"As you'd expect. But still, Vienna can afford to be a tart. It's surrounded by ageless culture, elegance personified by the aristocratic length of people's fingers and the scars cut into the cheekbones of the old men, scars from duels, real duels over real women." I draw my fingers below my eyes to show him where the marks are.

"Duels?"

"Oh sure. Viennese men will apparently still challenge other men to a duel. There are always reports about fraternity men getting carried away and shooting someone in the woods. So, in a city like that, you can imagine that North Americans stumble. I felt clumsy, stupid, cultureless. Just think, there are eighty museums and eighty-two libraries with eighteen million books, not to mention all the other stuff they've collected."

"How can you spout those statistics?"

"Well, I may be inventing them, but that's the effect of Vienna. It's so overwhelming that visitors carry away rafts of information. I spent a whole day in the Kunsthistorisches Museum, just looking for paintings of Judith with the severed head of Holofernes, paintings by Vouet, Liss, Cranach, Bloemaert, Solimena, Varotari, Saracini and Veronese."

"Whoa! Painters, right?"

"All painters, some greater than others. It's enough to stagger anyone, that labyrinth of connecting rooms, the marble staircase with Canova's *Theseus Slaying the Centaur,* two massive males struggling so that you can't tell which one is the monster. Everything in the city is textured with death, deliciously grotesque. It's so intense that after a while a person believes in ghosts. I actually expected to see Gustav Klimt and Sigmund Freud walking down a street together, arm in arm."

"They both lived there, I gather."

"They did. And since Freud worked there, it's probably no surprise that I always dream in Vienna, dreams full of mundane details, but disturbing, as if they're supposed to mean something to my real life. For example, last time I was there I dreamed that a stranger was opening my mail, but in the dream, I wasn't upset, didn't care. Because my intensely personal letters meant nothing to him. Actually, I can't remember if the invader was a man or a woman."

"Do you dream a lot when you travel?"

"Not usually. Although two weeks ago in Brussels—that's strange, I remember now—I had a vivid dream about Budapest. It's not that far from Vienna, you know, really two cities, Buda and Pest. The river runs between the castle on the hill and the newer city below. I was walking under the linden trees, which were shedding leaves onto the pathways. I was holding something in my hands, walking slowly and looking at my feet in an effort to understand how they moved without my thinking about them. Hmmm."

Derrick Atman is listening, looking straight into my eyes. "In one city you dream about being in another. What were you holding in your hands? Your life?"

"If you like. That won't make me change my mind."

He smiles. "Tell me more about Vienna."

"Everyone drinks coffee in Vienna, beautiful small cups of dense coffee. I can taste it now, a *kleiner Brauner*, with a small knobbled glass of water beside. Or thick floats of *Einspänner*, a long silver spoon standing in the foam. I was walking down Wahringerstrasse one evening, window-shopping, and I bumped into someone I hadn't seen for fifteen years, a fellow I'd dated briefly after high school. We hedged, defensive but curious. What were we doing in Vienna at the same time?"

"Presumably he enjoyed its macabre charms too."

I don't tell Derrick Atman, but I thought the old flame had potential as an assassin, although he turned out to be too self-conscious, too worried about his appearance to make a reliable killer. "We had coffee together, a *Fiaker*, coffee with rum, but we avoided telling each other what we were doing there. The city permits that kind of mystery. No one has to answer for anything, past lives or other secrets."

"It sounds like a play."

"As good as. We arranged to meet and go to the Freud Museum the next day, 19 Berggasse in the ninth district, but he didn't show up, so I went alone. Climbing those stairs, I could imagine what it would have been like to be a patient wanting an answer to my dreams, that was Freud's métier, interpreting dreams. But the penetrating stare that I attribute to Freud seemed absent, despite his hat and walking stick in the foyer. Only his steamer trunk looked vaguely promising. It was supposed to represent the baggage he took when he exiled himself from Austria in 1938. In the waiting room, I imagined being a patient, twisting on the stained chairs, desperate either to remember or forget."

He is watching me without a flicker of expression.

I go on. "I decided then that no therapy could cure me. The legs of the chairs seemed like unsprung traps, the potted palm was ominous, the table bent itself in a nervous arc and the worn Persian carpet over the scratched parquet floor held the nervous shufflings of the feet of a thousand nightmares. The consultation room was empty, the famous couch moved to London, so although I sat on the edge of one chair—you weren't supposed to touch the furniture, certainly not sit on it—I was unable to confess any of my paranoias or desires. And, no, I don't know if Klimt and Freud ever met, although, given their time, it's possible they did."

"Klimt?"

"You know, those gold-leaf women he painted, dark and hazy."

"I can't say as I do know."

"It doesn't matter. Vienna has that effect, it makes people hunt for mementos of death by remembering details. I would walk past the enormous complex of hospital buildings, the *Krankenhuisen*, and hear women crying, anguished wails. The hospital area was close to a whole broadsheet of graveyards, the *Hernalser Friedhof*, the *Dornbacher Friedhof*, the *Ottakringer Friedhof*. Peaceful. The *Zentralfriedhof*, the central cemetery, has almost six hundred acres with some three million graves, including transplanted remains—they were dragged back, you see—of Beethoven and Schubert. And then, of course, there's the *Friedhof der Namenlosen*, those who have no name, suicides and other bodies washed ashore from the Danube."

"Isn't Mozart buried there?"

"Somewhere. They don't know exactly. He was buried in a mass grave, common enough then, and nothing to do with the myth of how poor he was. That poor bastard lived in twelve different lodgings in ten years. Can you imagine the moving? Until finally he sweated his way to his own requiem in musty Rauhensteingasse. I always go there and sniff the rooms, although I refuse to go to Figarohaus. The CBC plays too much Mozart, and I am not about to have an orgasm at the thought of standing in the same room where both Haydn and Beethoven paid respectful visits. I'm more interested a street close to that, Blutgasse, named for the Knights Templar who were massacred there in 1312. So you see, it's a wonderful place, all that blood for a bland Canadian to dabble her fingers in."

"You're macabre."

"The better to hire you, my friend."

He snorts. "Go on. What about all those museums?"

"Well, there's an *Uhrenmuseum*, a time museum, with a thousand clocks all ticking and tocking their relentless way toward tomorrow, almost in line with the *Ankeruhr*, the animated clock on the Hoher Markt. That clock is high Art Nouveau, but it's like a children's musical. A host of rulers and their consorts, long since dead, with Joseph Haydn bringing up the rear, come stepping out every noon to parade above the market."

"Funny, that's how I imagine Europe, with musical clocks and men in pigtails and big tables of people sitting around eating legs of pork and drinking out of tankards."

"Like a Brueghel painting. You see, that's the difference between a place like Vienna and Calgary. Vienna was built on salt and music. And look at us, this city was built on oil and cattle and police, no romance in that origin."

"We are eating in what you said was once a sex shop."

"We're on the haberdashery side, but okay."

"But," and he leans back to let the waitress take away our empty plates—I have polished mine clean—"we don't have evidence of the same terrible grief, no war or famine."

"Or plague. There's a memorial to plague victims in the Graben, the *Pestsäule*, a baroque column of tortured bodies falling, climbing over one another, rending their death through a kind of stone cloud pillar. If you don't stop to look closely, the carved statue seems decorative. Then you see that the figures are racked with pain, their teeth bared, their bodies ravaged, writhing in death above a modern square of heart-lessly exclusive perfume shops and hairdressers. And we can't point to the exact spot where the gallows stood a mere hundred years ago. They can."

He searches my face, and I fear he can read how much I wanted to die there, in Vienna's shrouded eloquence, the crooked solemnity of cobbled streets.

"What about churches?" he asks. He seems to want to hear this catalogue, this enlistment of Vienna's excessive and never-ending waltz. I suppose he wants to delay me, but I'll indulge him. And talking about Vienna means that I don't have to exaggerate.

"Of course, Vienna's full of churches, and the churches are full of tombs with their inhabitants sculpted above their bones, waved toward heaven by tear-drenched angels. Tombs and arranged marriages. In the Augustinerkirche alone, Maria Theresa married François of Lorraine, Marie-Louise married Napoleon by proxy, and Franz Joseph, the last of the authentic Hapsburgs, married Elisabeth. There they were, vowing to fidelity—fat chance—while behind the grating in the far wall sat the fifty-four silver urns containing the embalmed but absolutely dead hearts of the imperial house. They're still there, everyone royal from 1637 to 1878. Now isn't that a great spot to swear until death do you part?"

His left hand holds his bandaged right, his chin resting on both, and he watches me with—I hardly dare interpret his expression—absolute delight. I've seduced him. He's taking pleasure in my obsessions. Not quick, hurry, let's get this nasty job done and be gone. Oh, he could have taught my other assassins so much.

I can't resist going on. "A priest told me that the chapel has to be guarded day and night. Apparently, people try to steal the urns, which are cemented into the floor. They scratch the silver, even pray to them as relics *now*, when skepticism about empire must be at its peak. And if they're disappointed by those urns, they can visit the catacombs beneath the Stephansdom because that's where the other organs and the entrails are embalmed, and—"

"Wait, you mean they actually cut up the bodies, put the hearts in one place and—"

"The entrails in another and the bones in another! The bones are in the *Kaizergruft* of the Kapuzinerkirche. Talk about spreading yourself around!"

"Maybe they wanted to ensure there would be some part of

their bodies left to contemplate, and they stood a better chance if they divided themselves up."

"I guess. The best of the three spots is really the Imperial Burial Vault in the Capuchin Church. Hapburgs have been encrypted there since 1633, and I guess it's still operative. The most recent sarcophagus is of the Empress Zita, who died in 1989."

"Can you go into it?"

"Oh yes. It's a tourist attraction. You ring an arthritic bell, then you're admitted by a reluctant doorkeep who seems to feel he has a right to inspect visitors before taking the entrance fee—you have to pay to be horrified—then you go down a steep flight of stairs, as if descending to a cellar under a cellar, all the while the smell of mildew and rot gets stronger and stronger. The air feels damp and metallic, as if particles of lead are flaking from the welded caskets."

"You mean there are caskets sitting there, not buried?"

"Sepulchral art, yes, but they're not caskets, more like enormous sarcophagi, elaborately cast metal casings. The crypt is spacious, almost an apartment, with a foyer and ante-chambers, careful excavations laid out like rooms. You stand there, clutching your jacket because it's chilly as hell, breathing the smell of damp stone and cold earth and moldering bones trying to fathom this place. I mean, we associate vaults with money and banking—as if they don't bury people—but this crypt is unbelievable. Here is the whole of imperial Vienna, lying side by side like bottles in a wine cellar, completely dead, but refusing to die."

"Refusing?"

"Well, one can hardly ignore such macabre statements. They planned their grave sites as deliciously as their cakes. And they run the gamut in size and grandeur. Joseph II, the one who introduced the hygienic practice of sack burials during the plague, has a plain copper box, but then Maria Theresa and her consort—they're buried together—have the most elaborate heap of lead and pewter you can imagine. It's cast as an enormous double bed, elaborated by hanging folds of drapery, grieving angels, crowned skulls, and there they are, statues semireclining above their remains, looking at each other with an expression that I could only read as amusement, almost as if they'll proceed to undress and have conjugal relations the moment the crypt door slams shut behind the last tourist!"

"Guarded by angels."

"Literally. Cast iron angels pointing toward heaven. Talk about encapsulated bones. Emperors surrounded by multiple wives, emperors killed in battle, emperors who died in bed, emperors who were murdered, all guarding their secrets. Emperor Maximillian of Mexico is there, and Marie-Louise, that unfortunate consort to Napoleon, both resting with their ancestors and their sculpted angels."

"No wonder you adore the city."

"Don't be sarcastic. But it's a wonderful relief to accept that excess. Even visiting the crypt seems normal."

"Do you think they dream?"

"Who? The emperors? Oh, they probably worry about letters held in state vaults, ready to fall into the hands of historians and rapacious readers. They were too early to visit Freud, to benefit from his interpretations."

"He seems appropriate."

"Oh yes, in Vienna, Freud makes absolute sense. And it doesn't stop at the crypt either. There's an Undertaking Museum that covers the history of funerals and embalming. I particularly enjoy that museum, although it's difficult to see. You have to call and make an appointment in advance. You know, every social class and every guild member had to be identified by a different pall, and the *Enterprise des Pompes Funèbres* decided whether a corpse would be accompanied by white or black horses. They were the ones who introduced reusable coffins to alleviate the expense of burial. And it was up to them to assuage the epidemic fear that people had of being buried alive. They had to ensure the dead were really dead, stabbed to the heart so they wouldn't wake up entombed, although there was even a solution for that unlikely possibility. The rich would arrange to be buried with a little cord hanging close to their hand so that if the corpse woke up, it could ring the bell with one tug, and a grave attendant would come running with a shovel and start to dig. Of course, I asked if this had ever happened, and the city employee conducting the tour nodded as solemnly, as if I'd asked him whether there were more deaths in winter than summer."

Derrick Atman's eyes are smiling, although he isn't laughing at me now. "Did you have to attend many funerals when you were a child?"

"No, none. That's why I'm so curious. And you know what I liked best? You'll laugh because I've told you how much I hate cameras. Before the dead were put into coffins, they propped them up in a chair for a photograph, one magnesium flash. Now that's what photographs should do. Reclaim the dead."

"Charming."

"*Memento mori!* Just a few steps from Schubert's *Sterbehuis*, where he raved and sang his delirious way to an end brought on by typhoid and syphilis."

"Nobody dies of that anymore."

"No," I say, taking a last swallow from my glass. "We have to purchase our dyings."

"Isn't there anything happy in Vienna?"

"Sure. There's a Circus and Clown Museum, but it's sad,

tinged with rancid greasepaint, tinsel and spangles. The *Wiener Kriminalmuseum*, the Criminal Museum, is much better, although it's operated by the police and full of stories about people driven to poison and stabbings. And there's a zoo, although I never went there."

"I thought they filmed—what?—Orson Welles' *The Third Man* in Vienna."

"They did, and you can still ride the *Riesenrad*, the ferris wheel built for the 1898 fair. It takes you up and around once, slowly, so you can practice being caught in a triangle of murder in one of those sedate cabins. It's in the Prater, the park, and after I rode the wheel, I walked and walked down the Hauptallee to the Lusthaus, a restaurant that could just as well be another *fin-de-siècle* crypt, for a coffee, first a *kleiner Brauner*, then a *Verlängerten*." I stop and he says nothing. I can hear him listening. "I've been talking far too much. Let's have some coffee."

"It will never live up to Vienna's."

"No, but then, I couldn't find the perfect assassin there either."

"Assassin." His face changes instantly, and he looks angry, genuinely angry.

"I'm sorry. I don't mean to offend you. It's a word I've been contemplating a lot lately. I guess you're more like an assistant, a care giver kind enough to ease my hurt."

I can tell from his voice that he is furious. "I am neither an assistant nor a practitioner of euthanasia. And assassin is too melodramatic. That should be reserved for those who murder famously and without compunction."

"I am sorry," I say more softly, meaning it this time.

He nods at the waitress. "Be careful about your assumptions. I'm a Quaker from Winnipeg. I am not your lover. And I have never been to Vienna."

WE ARE SILENT while we wait for our coffee. I keep staring at the now dark window of the woman's room, and he turns his water glass around and around. The waitress comes with cups, pours more water, offers dessert, which we decline, as if our hunger is over, terminated.

When she has left again, he says, making a visible effort, "And what about love then?"

"What about love?"

"Have you not known love, found love? Is there no one who will miss you, who will cry for you when you are no longer a voice or a body?"

I swallow hard, and now I am the one who is angry, a wash of clear adrenaline flooding up to my ears. "You mean, would I be asking for you to commit this injury against me if I were happily 'in love' now? Love has nothing to do with my decision, although love isn't easy to give up. It lodges where it will, like any trickster. Every time I thought I had found love, I found another assassin — sorry, killer."

"I know I'm not the first. By the time I'm called, people have usually tried several amateurs."

"Exactly. But even loved, why persist in thinking that love will prove a reason to continue? What if I am well loved, loved with attention and delight? Does that inoculate me against despair? Does love provide a home or erase restlessness?"

"It helps."

"Not at all. Love makes the terror worse, the desire to die more intense. Because it can persuade a person to accept the plunge of life, to tolerate the worst indignities."

"I gather that isn't your solution then. Have you been to Paris?"

I stare at him. Is he crazy? "Paris?"

"Yes, supposedly the most romantic city in the world."

"Paris? No, I've never been there. Wait, yes, I *was* there once, believe it or not, as a student. I'd clean forgotten. The famous Parisian parks were gravel, the children rolled hoops through a layer of dust that permeated everything, and the breakfast croissants were huge, chewy and full of grease. I remember the spectrum of color that radiated from the impressionist paintings in the Jeu de Pomme and how we bought frozen oranges to eat with a plastic spoon in the park. I suppose I was young enough to be hungry for love, but we were on a school trip, not there long enough to discover more than a few corners, visit the Tour Eiffel and the Left Bank."

"A school trip?"

"Strangely, yes. That was the one journey I made with a group of people, other students and a teacher who was in charge but who wanted to shop for fashions. Tante Katje insisted that I go, that it would be good for my French, although it made no discernible difference in my ability to speak that language. I remember standing alongside my school-mates feeling as if we did not come from the same world. I wanted to be alone, I wanted to linger and loiter and measure the size of the light and the misty rain alone. I imagine I still fancied that I could have an impact on my own life. I must have believed that when I actually touched the hand of some-one who could guess my inarticulate dreams, that touch would be electric, uncompromised, full of meaning."

"So you were ready to fall in love."

"I watched and wandered and sniffed at the dirty Seine, thinking my patience would reward me. I wanted to be surprised, seduced by an outrageous recognition. I was waiting for a touch beyond touch, a breath to inflame me. All I learned was that Paris was the wrong stage for discovery, too mythologized, too adamantly romantic. Paris was full of pilgrims, itinerants like the students I was with, lurking on its fringes. If I wanted to be part of a collage, I could tear myself to pieces, but I wanted to be whole when love reached for me, I wanted to have faith in my surrender. I imagined being burned by a gaze, I imagined smothering my conscience in hot steam, but I could not imagine myself as painter's model or sad inspiration. Maybe I just missed the prairies."

"You were disappointed."

"I was a teenager, too young to be a widow, and without crescents of paint under my fingernails."

"So much for romance then."

"I do not remember Paris because I learned later, from less romantic cities, that when I do reach out, I touch the sleeves of killers."

⌐

"For example, one of my would-be lovers gave me a copy of Jung. Why Jung, I wondered, with his belief in polygamy for men, his advice to women to settle for religion rather than passion. Jung. Wouldn't you say that was a Freudian action?"

"You're very funny, you know." He is smiling, his whole face alight.

"Oh, I don't think so."

"Sad people often are."

"Funny?"

"Yes."

"And what about now?"

"Now?"

"Yes, now, this moment."

My dear one is working right now, guarding the sleep of children who fight disease and debilitation, who have a right to be unhappy but who struggle on.

When I close my eyes at night, draperies shift behind them. A hand reaches out and fails to impart a touch. A voice repeats and repeats an indecipherable phrase, trying to persuade me not to flinch. I turn within the twisted sheets of dreams, dreams that sandpaper my life and will not let me rely on love.

My dear one will refuse to believe my abandonment, and he will go on loving me, even after he has turned his face toward forgetting.

My gentle lover, who refused to become my assassin.

Now I sigh, shrug, avoid Derrick Atman's eyes. "Shall we go?"

"Surely." We settle the bill between us, and then he pulls on his gloves carefully, as if afraid to make too sharp a motion with his hurt hand.

He brings my coat, holds it while I slip my arms into the sleeves. Knotting the belt, I look around the restaurant, the diners huddled together in their jigsaw of conversation.

Here I have finished my last meal, settled my last hunger.

ON THE STREET again, he tucks my hand under his arm, my own glove next to his.

"Walk a little more?"

I feel fuzzy from talking too much, from the wine, the warmth, the food. The mild chinook wind, cobweb soft, lifts my hair, pushing under the roots. "All right. Let's walk to the river."

Silent, we walk north, following the street, crossing the rapid transit tracks, until we meet Chinatown, then west a few blocks, around the Chinese Cultural Centre and the scrawl of Eau Claire Market. Past restaurants and bars, noisy groups of drinkers celebrating chinook. Beyond the market we cross the bridge to Prince's Island, the city's noise a murmuring now, and walk along the edge of the Bow River, from one pool of occasional light to another, until we find a relatively dry bench. The river is groaning with thaw. The ice will soon push itself away from the banks and begin to canoe east.

We sit. We listen.

I SOUGHT PLACES famous for their suicides, I looked for a city that would open its arms to me, bear me away without malice or undue scrutiny. I found cities full of weather, faces perplexed by centuries of dust, decades of car exhaust, as if drizzle's breath were a character, a silent witness to the gentle death of stone and mortar.

And here I am in Calgary. Home again.

AT LAST HE asks me the question I have been waiting for.

"Why here then, why here when you could choose any city anywhere, when you could have done this well and truly abroad, where accident would be assumed, where no one would question, where someone else could take care of the details. But here?"

"Look, if you want out, just say so. Of course, you'll owe *me* the kill fee."

"No, I won't back out. That would be unprofessional. But I'm sad that you want to do this. Some deaths, you know, are good deaths. People who are desperate or suffering deserve to die with dignity. But you, I'm—okay, I'm furious that you—your funny life, your stories . . . What about Tante Katje? What about the friends who love you? What about him?"

I sit staring at the river, stoic, refusing to let his words touch my determination. "This is about me. And being here seems necessary. This is the only home I ever knew as home."

"IT'S STRANGE, BUT I am more homesick here than when I am away. I looked for a place famous for suicides, hoping such a place would teach me how to carry out my own. Trieste, for certain. San Francisco too, but I couldn't die in the States. Too common, too vulgar, too commercial. I searched for a place without a history, a pastless moment, a set of streets that gathered together the secrets of the future, hope without embarrassment. What an impossible task."

"Well, the United States is the only country that practices unembarrassed hope. We know all about Americans, the Gatsbys and the Supermans and the Mulders."

I can't help chuckling. "The first time I took a quivering airplane south to Las Vegas, I thought I might meet suicide there. The plane was full of weekenders dying to lose money, the airport brisk with shy gamblers, bustling tourists with their pockets full of nickels. Such terrible anticipation."

"Well, Vegas is a gambler's paradise. Although I've never been there."

"Vegas is a city that has decided to imitate the past, but on a manageable scale, an entire city false-fronted and composed for a movie set. What's poignant about Vegas is its crayoned color, as if the subtle shades of the desert need to be driven back, kept at bay. I landed there in the deep hot night and took a cab, festooned with advertisements for escort agencies, to the MGM Grand."

"The movie company runs a hotel there?"

"I don't know who runs it, but it's all based on Dorothy and the Wizard of Oz. I suppose I was the wrong guest because I didn't understand the references. Inside the green-tinged glass—the Emerald City, you see—the lights were hallucinatory. To get to the actual guest rooms, you had to wend your way through four different casinos. Every hotel in Las Vegas has more than one casino now—you can choose to gamble in different decors, depending on the aura that you want to surround yourself with. So to get to my room, I walked, literally, a yellow brick road, past newsstands and all-night bars, past plastic emeralds and other strange pieces of Oz that didn't quite mesh. I felt as if I'd been sleeping and was remembering the story through some twilight dream. After not quite a mile of yellow brick road, there was a double door, locked, which required my guest card, and behind it the hushed plush of hotel space, rooms with brass numbers and brass doorknobs, a sleek elevator, the noise of coins falling into metal jaws remote as water. When I could finally lift my feet to the bed and look up at the ceiling, I knew I had wandered into a playpen, and a playpen is not the most suitable place to die."

"You deliberately went there to commit suicide?"

"Well, in a mythological way, it seemed like a good place, so shallow, so desperately gullible."

"And when you realized that you were not going to die, you decided to stay and have a good time, to play."

"Well, it is a playpen."

"Did you gamble?"

I have to laugh at him, the serious look on his face when he asks that question. "Of course. The first slot machine I tried, I put in a penny and won two-hundred and sixty pennies. I had dreamed that exact event a few months earlier, so I already knew what the sound of those pennies rumbling into the trough was like."

"You dream a lot."

"Even if I don't know what my dreams mean."

He sees that I have saddened and wants to distract me. "Tell me more about Vegas."

"Well, so there I was in the Emerald City, in a functional hotel room, alone and unable to take the four kinds of sleeping pills I had brought, unable to imagine perpetual sleep in a place that refuses to name sleep, in a city that insists on nightless night. If the place hadn't been a shrine to free-wheeling capitalism, it would have been surreal. I went out, restless, thirsty, and in the dusty heart of that imaginary town, I searched for the despair that I assumed I had merely mislaid. And found nothing but low ceilings and felt-covered tables, relentlessly cheerful faces. It was frightening to discover that the playfulness was contagious—I felt remarkably jubilant, at home in my jeans and my cowboy boots. I hiked the strip, from the far beacon of the Luxor to New York, New York to Fantasy Island to Caesar's Palace, all the worlds that no one traveler could ever visit perched side by side, miniaturized, distorted. The strip is in a state of constant renovation. The old hotels are being blown up so that theme parks can replace naves of corridors and trysts of mourning."

"Reduced?"

"Oh, and vulgar. Such astonishing vulgarity, daring to believe in itself."

"And then?"

"Well, I gambled. Of course I did. I won two-hundred and sixty pennies, then I won about forty dollars in a quarter machine, and then I sat on the lower level of what the Luxor pretends is a replica of the Great Pyramid and played black-jack until that forty dollars was gone. The machines were friendly, greedy but polite. The cool light, the hyperventilated air, I could imagine I was in a crypt, which made it impossible to kill myself. For I was already entombed, and my gesture would have been redundant."

"You changed your mind."

"I enjoyed myself. Like a kid, I gaped and I wandered, I gawked and I plunked quarters into machines here and there, without expecting dividends, just for the sound of the whirling tumbrels, the lemons and the stars trying to outspin each other. I delivered the parcel I was couriering—some kind of pharmaceutical formula, I think—the next morning, drove it to the outskirts, to an elegant phalanx of office buildings, then drove back and had the valet at the Emerald City park my rental again. I walked up the yellow brick path, had a wonderful lunch of cornmeal pancakes and decided to concede that the city was only for fun."

"Didn't you go anywhere else?"

"I took the rental out one day, drove into the terra cotta desert and walked, watching lizards and brandishing cacti, the hot red light lifting my feet. I felt—warm. Good."

"Good."

"Well, I was in make believe. It's hard to hang on to sadness when you can hide in play land."

"So you decided to live."

"I decided it was pointless to die there. The sheer undulating energy wouldn't let me hesitate. I had to keep up with the gambling. "

"I've heard all the drinks are free."

"Not quite, but you know, there are no minibars in the hotel rooms in Vegas. They don't want you to drink in your room; they want you to go downstairs to the bars, surrounded by the sounds and calls of winning. It's the only place I've been that doesn't put overpriced liquor in little fridges. So I'd brought all my sleeping pills, but I didn't have any gin to wash them down."

"You could have bought a bottle somewhere."

"I suppose."

"And you were happy until you left?"

"I was euphoric. The night before I was due to fly home, I managed to get a ticket to Cirque de Soleil. Do you know them? They're a famous circus troupe from Québec, brilliant contortionists, gymnasts, acrobats."

"I've heard. They don't use animals."

"Just humans. It's always easier to get a ticket if you're a single, so I managed to get in to a virtually sold-out show. It was one of those nights when I felt as if I could suspend my body from their aerial sweep, the troupe were so marvelously agile, so adept at enfolding the watchers in their illusion. And they were full of laughter, clowning, shouts of pleasure opened up by the expressiveness of their limbs. Like any circus, the players were inscrutable. You couldn't see individual faces. But there was one clown, a woman, who did stand out. She had deliberately made herself resemble Pippi Langstrump—you know, Pippi Longstocking, that wily character whose father was a pirate and who knew how to survive on the high seas. A Canadian might imagine Anne of Green Gables but with attitude. Anyway, that figure of the pig-tailed, red-headed miscreant girl is recognizable enough, and she's always been one of my favorites, a version of what I would like to be."

He nudges me with his elbow.

"Wish I had been. Anyway, this clown carried her antics into the audience, bridged the invisible zone between stage and seats, teasing, seating people in the wrong places, messing up well-combed hair. She made people clutch themselves with laughter, but she also terrified them. Wouldn't you be afraid if you expected to be entertained, if you expected to be able to remain safely at a distance from the smell of circus grease, and then found a pig-tailed tramp pulling off your tie?"

"I might be relieved."

"Not most people. They were afraid of her. They hoped she would leave them alone, even while they rolled in their seats at other people's discomfort."

"Yes, we don't want to be the cause of laughter."

"But I wanted her to touch me with her quick transformations. I wanted her to come to me."

"And?"

"She would not. She scanned the audience, she looked at me, she saw me, she looked directly into my eyes, and she averted hers. She moved to the other side of the aisle, she played her monkey trick on a blonde in a leather skirt."

"You think that was deliberate?"

"Oh yes, it was. She shunned me."

"Because you were sad?"

"Because I was a lost cause, a dead soul."

"How could she see that?"

"I don't know. She looked at me, and a wince of rejection crossed her face. I waited afterward by the stage door, willed myself to wait and watch for her. She came out, slipped by without her wig of red hair, assuming I would not recognize her, but I did, I knew her gait, her quick-footed movement, and I lurked behind her through the corridors of that hotel's casino to another set of those magic entrances, where she inserted her card into the private slot and vanished, the door swinging behind her as if to send me away."

"What did you do?"

"I stood there in her hotel corridor, and I cried. I cried and cried, knowing I could not finish my self-erasure in Vegas, but I was still locked out of its gorgeous midway. I had been prohibited. I went back to my hotel, packed, lay awake on the comfortable cool-sheeted bed and waited for the next day. She had immobilized me. No planes leave Vegas in the morning. The flight was the next evening, and I had to kill the day, erase my own waiting. I lay there, wide awake, until check-out time the next morning, then left my bag with the bellhop and paced the sidewalks, the tawdry malls, liquor stores and cheap trinkets for sale, the leafleteers handing me advertisements for strip shows and animal performances and terrible murders, and me, not only could I not commit suicide, but I could not tumble into the pleasures of the carnival. The barkers, the Mexican gardeners, the bartenders, all had a place in this circus, and I was shut out."

"Why did that trouble you so much?"

"Because I thought it was a heartless city, that it wouldn't care if I died there. And even worse, I always thought that when I could no longer stand the mundane necessities of delivering items, courier to the world, handing over a manifest for the recipient to sign, I would join the circus, make people like me laugh."

"A common enough dream, although there are hardly many circuses left."

"Oh, there are midways, sideshows, astrology fairs. Someone always needs a girl to hold a scarf."

"And you—"

"She made it clear that I had no future, that joy and make believe are beyond what I can accomplish."

"So back you went to the pyramids."

"How did you know?"

"From tumble to tomb."

"Do you think the gamblers and tourists who swarm the Luxor know its story, can even imagine its haunting?"

"How can the Luxor be haunted? The real pyramids are in Egypt."

"Oh, I don't think you can take such a loaded site and re-create it without some quiver in the spheres, without some force trailing along to ensure a meddlesome watcher. Yes, I went back to the Luxor, found a high stool and played poker against a machine that refused to deal me a single ace. I lost my courier fee. I left the stool, paced the pyramid's perimeter. I stood in a shop fingering a silk scarf printed with the feet of King Tut, I took the boat ride through the grotto and the river Styx, I went back to my stool, which someone else had taken over, found another a few machines away and perched, feeding quarters to its quick mechanical dealings. I lost a week's pay. I wandered again, pulled up to a counter and stirred a frothy cappuccino—good coffee is easy to find in casinos, they want people to stay awake—even bought a package of cigarettes and lit one, but I was in a grave and I could not escape its chilled slow exhalation of decay."

"It can't resemble the real pyramids."

"Of course not. The smell of the real pyramids is alive with death, the taint of a living tomb, even empty. The glass imitation in Vegas is filled to the brim with holiday clothes, cosmetics, belts, amulets. White and whole-grain breads, jars of what they think resembles Egyptian food, decorate the multiple restaurants. All things that the dead require. If you look closely, you notice the gamblers' faces painted with green malachite. And there are statues everywhere, both breathing and cardboard, of women, promising companionship in some version of a hereafter. It is only too ghastly a reproduction of those eager and elaborate graves, those hallowed burial chambers. The windows of a pyramid view the promising sunrises of eternity. What quarries, I could only wonder, invented that glass and steel iniquity? I imagined the architect presented with this task, his euphoria wrestling with his night sweats. I imagined him visiting Cairo in order to make an excursion to Giza, his shock at the pure tonnage of blocked stone."

"You've been there too?"

"I once spent a Christmas in Cairo."

"Christmas?"

"It was when matters between Egypt and Israel were still tense, but unbelievably the two countries were beginning to speak, well, more like whisper to each other. Everyone had lost children in the war, and those losses made them touch hands, briefly enough. I had to deliver some material for a telephone company; they were trying to find a way to connect the two countries again."

"Cairo."

"I gather you've never been there."

"No, I told you, my circulations are largely North American."

"It swarms with smell, Cairo, for all that it is dry, arid."

"The Nile, Cairo, it seems—"

"Exotic. Yes, in the way that we deodorized North Americans make exotic a place with a story beyond our imaginings. Cairo is noise and tumult, passion and ritual and a veiled glance wrapped around congestion. I saw very few veils, although now I understand that they are coming back, the political erotics of women's faces. It was sultry on the streets, but wildly prayerful. Muezzins interrupted the more assiduous noise of cars and braying donkeys."

"You make it sound a melee."

"It was, although my memory is certainly faulty. I remember odd things vividly, the corner money changers, the smell of charcoal grills on the streets, the lift of cloth over the groins of men wearing galabias. The Egyptian museum where I spent an afternoon. The display cases were coated with dust, stunningly precious artifacts lay almost neglected, open to the gaze of intruders. It was that combination of carelessness and generosity that struck me. Sadat had just been assassinated. There were bomb scares galore, soldiers with Russian AK guns on every corner, in every alley and street, and yet I felt so utterly safe that I wondered at my own stupidity. What was I missing, foolish me? What did I not comprehend, so oblivious to the signs that others intuitively knew?"

"You were in danger?"

"Probably. And I didn't believe it, I refused to be sensible about what I should have known. I wasn't stoned or robbed, I wasn't offered camel rides or the services of someone's sister or brother. I was accosted by innumerable money changers who offered to sell me Egyptian pounds for American dollars, which I didn't have. And the warm white-toothed smile of the driver who slipped into the stream of the streets as if the car were swimming, the Klaxon horns a symphony rather than a complaint."

"And you went to the pyramids."

"Oh yes, I had that same driver take me to Giza, made sure that my legs and my arms were decently covered, although I could not brighten my paleness and the inquisitive western shape of my sunglasses. The camels yawned their cavernous mouths, the camel drivers and dragomen lounging around the pyramids looked at me with justifiable scorn. A woman alone is never auspicious. But my guide (the brother of the beautiful driver) insisted that it was not enough to look at the outside. The pyramid of Chephren was open, we had to visit the chamber of the sarcophagus."

"Inside?"

"Inside. The passage we crawled through was black, a steep climb in a space so narrow it was impossible to turn, and I felt my lungs constricting, my eyes straining through the lantern light."

"Lantern?"

I hear my own hollow chuckle. "You see, in such excursions we transport ourselves to the era we think appropriate. Of course, there were no lanterns, the passage was strung with a weak loop of electric bulbs, ugly and dim, although it felt more like lantern light to me. The guide went ahead, encouraging me as we proceeded, for I was ready to turn back, the fetid air wrapped itself around my throat, my eyes, even blocked my ears with dust. And strange distortions of sense took place. I believed we were ascending, but my guide informed me that we were descending. Perhaps luckily, I could not turn around."

"You couldn't turn around?"

"No, the passage was literally too tight."

"And when you reached the center?"

"It was a great empty stone room that did not even echo."

"No hint of the spirits of those buried alive?"

"None."

"So you had no wish to die there."

"I hadn't yet confronted my desire to die. By the time we reached the interior chamber, I was congested rather than afraid. And I admired my guide, who kept me going, kept me alive, entertained me with tales of how Caliph Manum had broken the passage open with fire and vinegar, how various adventurers had encountered their worst nightmares and died of terror, how bats as large as eagles used to nest in the passages, how stones were judiciously positioned to crush the bones of intruders. His stories in that stone vagina were strangely comforting, almost as if we were trapped in an Arabian night. I was his audience, but I knew I was also another tale to add to his store, and so I felt obliged, once we had reached the central room with its stone altar centered as obvious as a bed, to faint."

"You?"

"Yes, I fainted. He was ecstatic, lifted me to the stone slab, so that lying there I'm sure I imitated the position of the person whose final resting place it was. I woke to his warm hands chaffing my hands and feet, and when I opened my eyes, he revived me with small swallows of a strange palm juice from his thermos. It was, oddly enough, an industrial-type steel thermos of the sort that miners carry in Canada."

"Did he recommend you to God?"

"No, he was too aware of irony to go that far. But he did advise me, with tremendous solemnity, not to lick the stone on which I lay for fear I would be deafened. At least, I think he said deafened. Which made me want to do exactly that, and when he was bending down to gather up his torch and thermos, quick as a cat, I did. Nothing happened. I could hear as well as ever. I asked him if I could take a small pebble that shone on the otherwise clean-picked floor, and when he agreed to look away—for you're not to take so much as a crumb of stone—I surreptitiously put the pebble in my mouth, held it under my tongue as we returned through the tight passage to the blinding sun of the outer world. I suspect now that my guide knew very well that I would want that souvenir and that he planted the pebble so as to give me hope."

"Hope?"

"Perhaps I was already sad."

"And the stone?"

"I carry it with me. Do you want to see it?"

"Please."

I reach into my purse, into the small side pocket. I have carried the stone for close to fifteen years, its small pocked surface rough against my fingers. "Here."

He holds out his hand and rolls the pebble in his palm, shields it from his breath as though it were a flame. And looks up to smile at me in the same way I reached for the guide's smile when we emerged from the cold relish of limestone into the Egyptian sun, when my driver's car slid away and I turned to watch the pyramids receding through the rear window. Without asking, they took me to the edge of the Nile, to a tourist café, for mint tea. We sat together, watching children patting their hands in the dust, watching fellucas tilt their sails on the river's glass. We sat together and I listened to the rustle of papyrus rushes.

"You didn't go deaf from licking the stone inside the pyramid."

"It came to me years later that he hadn't said I would be deafened, but that I would be deadened."

"So he was right."

"What do you think? Anyway, he asked me gently if I was recovered, and I felt immensely cherished."

"You have been fortunate," Derrick Atman says.

And I feel I must subdue a snort of laughter. Fortunate. "To have crawled into a pyramid and fainted?"

"To know the difference between a pyramid of the imagination and a pyramid of the desert. The real thing."

"As if," I say sadly, "anything were. But it's getting chilly. Shall we walk back?"

I DO NOT tell him that I watched them flailing barley, the women beating the stalks as if to punish them, dust rising into already dusty air and the canvas that held the grain whipping upward to winnow the chaff. I stood in that remote village, on the unclear edge between Egypt and the Sudan, and smelled the caramel smell of malt, let the dust settle on my bare arms.

I was staring at bread and its becoming. I should have fainted then.

WE TURN AND begin to walk slowly across the island toward the mitered skyline, our strides matching.

"All these places you've been to," he muses. "Do you ever wonder how cities come to be where they are?"

"Accident, mostly. Amazing how cultural and political centers spring from swamps or deadfall."

"And yet enshrine their location."

"Well, that's easy with seaside towns, Vancouver and Kiel, Sydney and Tofino."

"Tofino?"

"Not really a city. Just a little resort village on the western shoulder of Vancouver Island. You should go there for a visit sometime. Take your mind off your work. I make a pilgrimage there every year, the farthest west coast of Canada, crowded with cedars and the splash of endless rain. That's the edge of the world, a place to contemplate silence while the sea breaks on the beach."

"Why don't you go there now?"

"Because I'm afraid I've lost the ability to hear that peaceful roar." I won't tell him that if I go there expecting to be saved, I'll betray the tide rising and falling, the waves individual and momentary as blown glass. Virginia Woolf's "lemon-colored sailing boats" don't sail there. On that shelf of ocean riffs only gray metal tugs and great lumbering shipping vessels scout the horizon far from the rocks of the shore, passing the selvage of Canada as if it were invisible. You can hardly call such an expanse a view, only sweep, the quick race of sandpipers on the damp shore, gray clouds racing for krill, and the water breaking malachite against the rocks.

"What do you do there?"

"Step barefoot onto the balcony to hear the water, test the damp air, light a fire, stare into space." I always stay in Number 26, in a brown shingled building humble under the wind-bent trees. Last year, my dear one moved the dining table so we could watch the sea when we sat up to eat. The air smells of cedar, the crisp red smell that makes fires crackle and spit.

"Have you taken your lover there?"

My dear one. "Once," I say. "But when I lost the shape of the surrounding islands, when I could not dream the sound of tide, I knew I was losing ground."

"But you won't gain ground by hiring me."

"Oh yes, I will. A different slope of ground."

"DID YOU EXPECT the world to provide you with asylum?"

"No, I know there's no escape. I've learned there's no safety anywhere."

"Anywhere."

"You think people can transform themselves if their surroundings are right?"

"Yes, possibly."

"Listen, I refuse to leave the mud and the hurt and the garbage behind. I will not walk past a crying woman thinking of philosophers who ignored the hunger and cold around them. This sordid world surrounds me, and it is inside me. That is enough."

"You believe that every person needs to feel responsible for every dreadful injustice there is?"

"Why not?"

"The average person resists uncomfortable knowledge. No one deliberately sets out to visit landscapes of fear. Adventure, challenge, maybe, but downright fear?"

"People don't dare to make themselves afraid, just like they don't have the imagination to get themselves killed. Sure, masochists are boring people, they can even dull terror. Watch me watching these refugees. Watch me watching a hurricane. Watch me experiencing grief and horror by extension. But let me walk away without stepping in the vomit."

"You're cruel."

"No, I'm honest. So far as I'm concerned it's impossible to be neutral."

"But you don't have to deny the world's misery to live.

"Everyone else is living, but I am watching. They're swinging umbrellas on the way to work, they're eyeing a menu, they're telephoning someone who wants to hear their voice."

"You just did a few of those things."

"Sure. I know. But I'm inept. I have no hope. I'm tired. I want to sleep. Your job is to help me."

"We have all night."

"You're trying to see through me. You're trying to change the plot."

"No. I'm curious. I am always intrigued by what constitutes — despair."

"Then you do know why I've hired you. Don't you ever get tired of questions?"

He stops and faces me, puts both his gloved hands on my shoulders. "Look, I just want to know your story."

"Why bother?"

"Because it will help me make a better kill."

WE PASS THE wood-frame building of 1886, a huddled hen between newer bars and restaurants.

"That's an odd place," he gestures. "What is it?"

"The old Eau Claire and Bow River Lumber Company office. It's an all-day breakfast place now, not trendy, but they serve scrambled eggs at three in the afternoon."

"It looks mysterious there, different from all these new buildings."

"A good place to practice necromancy, probably the only place around."

"Necromancy?"

"Yes, communication with the dead. It's difficult here — the city's too recent, too determined to be picturesquely seedy to be seedy when it needs to be."

"Why does a city have to be seedy to communicate with the dead?"

"Every place should know the possibility of addiction. A city needs to know how to make its citizens repress a shudder."

"Danger, you mean?"

"Oh that, and experience too. Before they respect a place, people need to believe that it harbors unimaginable events."

"Ghost stories."

"If you will. For instance, ghosts in Belgium have solidity. They show themselves to strangers, they insist on appearing to people who cannot grasp their history and who don't know how to speak with them."

"As a defense?"

"Possibly. I try to follow the footsteps of ghosts. They have a distinctive shuffle."

"Visible sound, invisible people?"

"Hey, that's good. At least here the walls don't wear plaques, that patina of do-gooderness that you read in Toronto or London, endlessly blue-noting the famous people who slept under an obscure roof for five minutes."

"I haven't been to Toronto."

"You told me. By contrast, everything remotely famous or historical in Calgary is buried under a heavy glaze of concrete, usually a road. Imagine what archeologists of the year 3000 will say about us, how we loved shiny glass, polished stone, obsidian masks. Oil caps as fetish objects, no gardens or baths."

"It almost sounds like you believe in the deception of permanence."

"That life will continue, that breathing will go on, year after year? Yes, I believe that."

"Surely not."

"Why not?"

"Because every altered particle alters everything around it. If you are not here, how can you prescribe an imaginary permanence?"

I shrug. "You're not convincing. This place doesn't need me."

"Your leaving will alter the city's genes."

"A city has a different biology than a person."

We can hear the faint rumble of a freight carrying darkness along Ninth.

"And a railway runs through it," he muses.

"Well, railways run through most towns. But other cities turn their backs on railway tracks, make them backdrop to row housing and cross-hung wash lines, a division between right and wrong."

"Calgary seems a cheerful friendly place."

"Oh, it pretends to be friendly, doggishly friendly, so friendly that it's alarming, like a hyperactive child who can't stop himself from whirling in circles until he has to throw up."

"But it's not a calculating city."

"Oh no, it could never manage that. Much as it longs to try. Why do you think they put up such glorious gravestones?"

"How early does Calgary go to bed?"

"It depends on the night. And where you want to keep yourself awake. Weekdays it stops at a reasonable hour; people have to work in the mornings. But weekends, you can stake out Cowboys until at least three, and there are speakeasies that keep themselves wound up long past the time that anyone should want to be awake. I'm not a late-nighter myself. Are you?"

"I like a wander and a prowl after eleven. It clears the head, makes a person remember the excitement of night."

"You don't sleep well then?"

"Hardly. I wake up, I listen to the CBC International Service until I fall asleep again."

"That's strange. I listen to the same. When I can't sleep, those accented voices soothe me into my traveling mode."

"So when you're away from home you can sleep?"

"Oh, I sleep with a depth that would astonish you. It's only here I can't sleep."

"Why don't you go out then?"

"Profligate behavior at home. Much easier to do in other countries in a language I don't understand."

I don't tell him about how I would rather lie awake beside my dear one than sleep, that I have stored up enough touch to take me into the longest sleep of all.

THE GLAZE OF streetlights has taken on a yellow cast, and now our footfalls are separate sounds; fewer people and cars pass. He has a longer stride than I do, his feet hit the sidewalk with a neat precision that, were I not so relieved by his meticulousness, I would consider deadly. The air feels like a warm sponge moving across the body, snow-eater blowing through the hollow flutes of buildings with an infectious gaiety. Down the long reach of First Street, across from the Alberta Hotel building, where an all-night coffee bar still hovers with light.

"You know," I say, "that hotel used to be have the longest bar in the world."

"The longest bar? In the world?"

"I'm probably exaggerating. Maybe the longest bar in Canada. Maybe the longest bar in Alberta." But I stop, point it out to him, hesitated by renovation, the sad shift of lost time caught in its crumbling blocks. In the building behind us, artists' studios hum toward dawn. Against the higher blocks of Petro Canada and Gulf Canada, the silly crest of the Calgary Tower, these sandstone buildings hunker down into their own knowledge, refuse to hand over their ghosts, outwait time.

There, across the corner, is the Palliser again. The light turns green, and I feel the wind lift inside my collar, as if to say good-bye, the last time I will touch the chinook.

It no longer matters if my pubic hair is straight or kinky, if my nails are ragged, if my earrings match my shoes. My passport has been stamped for the last time, and my lungs will keep, before they collapse, a little of the exhilarating rush of wind that has lifted and swooped its way east across the Rockies.

THE DOORMAN, HIS top hat and tails fluttering in the wind, recognizes us and spins the door. "Did you have a good dinner?"

We nod, smile as we mount the pink-veined granite steps, absorb the hush of the lobby, still gleaming with expectation, but settling down for the night, the restaurant closing, the desk clerk suppressing a yawn.

"A nightcap?" Derrick Atman gestures toward the Oak Room.

"Why are you postponing the inevitable?"

"I'm not—just enjoying your company."

I know he is trying to keep me talking, but my veins buzz with the wine and the food and the river and the chinook. I feel as clear and transparent as Waterford crystal. "All right. Just one."

We cross the high-arched entrance into the mahogany and green room, settle in a corner, ease our legs out from a couch under a grouping of the Big Four. Derrick Atman removes his gloves again and chafes his hands together.

"I'm sorry. You were getting cold."

He smiles. "The tour was worth it. Seeing the river, smelling its thaw."

The waitress has tried to clip her unruly hair into a roll, strands escaping down the back of her neck. But her uniform is the standard penguin front, black-with-white formality as soothing as her stance with the tray.

He looks up at her, then at me. "Dorcas, what would you like?"

It's foolish to say that my heart stops, that I feel as if I have been dropped from an airplane. He hasn't said my name all night, although he knows it well enough, the file tells him the facts, he knows all about me and even more since I've served him so many stories embroidered with detail. But now that he has said my silly inappropriate name, I feel recognized, as if that oddly Biblical apparition I've been saddled with forever, the saintly Dorcas, is escapable at last. I gulp, try to fathom what might work best. "A glass of water."

"Nothing else?"

"Oh—you go ahead."

"Scotch," he says. "Macallan's if you have it."

"And," I fumble for this hemlock, surely what I choose now will be symbolic, my body will know the color and aroma of a final drink—"tea with Benedictine."

He chuckles as the waitress leaves, reaches to pat my hand. "You want the Benedictines as witness?"

"Not really, I—it just tastes good with tea."

"Monks are probably better at distilling liqueur than they are at resolving lives."

"I don't know much about monks. Although I stayed at a monastery once. There were no hotels in the area where I had to deliver a packet—I think they were seeds. I had a hell of a time with German customs persuading them that they contained no agricultural dirt, but I found myself in this remote part of the Black Forest with only a monastery to check into."

"And—?"

"It was eerie. I arrived in late afternoon, miles from nowhere, or so it seemed, and wandered around looking for some kind of door. The place was profoundly, solemnly enclosed, and I couldn't find an entrance until I ducked into an anteroom to an enormous kitchen, banging with heat and ladles, where a monk—and he was dressed in a black frock, truly—solemnly offered me a key and demanded payment in advance. Then he walked me along a maze of corridors to my room and pointed out the bathroom and toilet down the hall, making it very clear that I was not to communicate with anyone."

"Were you the only guest?"

"No, there were two others, student backpackers who were working their way south as the fall advanced. We ate in the refectory with the monks, everyone silently spooning pumpkin soup. It was a somber meal, served and eaten silently, although the students argued in low voices about which route to take, where they were likely to get a ride. She wanted to try major roads, the Autobahn, and he kept repeating that he wanted to hitch authentic roads. As if the Autobahn isn't authentic to Germany."

"Was the pumpkin soup good?"

"Delicious, although I found the bread too yeasty."

"Odd. Usually the bread at monasteries is very good, and the soup suffers—lumps, too much salt."

I look at him to see if he is joking, catch a twinkle to the lines around his eyes. He's teasing me, treating my discontent as a behavior, as if he knows me well. The waitress brings his Scotch, my pot of tea, the snifter of Benedictine, and for a few minutes we sit, warming our hands on the vapors.

I decide to tease him in return. "Do you visit monasteries often then?"

"Hardly, although occasionally a bed-ridden occupant will be given permission to die earlier than expected. But go on."

"Well, I tried to go for a walk, but the dark settled quickly. It was fall and frosty, the fog hung so close to the ground that I felt I was wading through clouds. I got chilled, didn't have a warm enough jacket and I wasn't sure where I was, so I gave up, went back to the room. I had trouble finding it, had to search all kinds of low-hanging hallways before I finally got my bearings."

"Are you easily misdirected?"

"Not usually. Maybe I was curious and needed an excuse to explore. There were Bible verses chalked over all the doors, and I was intrigued, wondered if they were meant to have a talismanic effect. My room—I should remember, I think I even scrawled it down—had something from Job."

"Trials and tribulations."

"I guess. The room itself was what you'd call Spartan, bare, the floor stone, the walls whitewashed, with one ladder-back chair and only a plain wooden crucifix nailed over the bed. I tried to sit up with my book, but I was shivering so much I finally gave up and climbed into bed, although it was no later than eight. The covers were folded over the end of the bed, but I couldn't get warm, and I lay there, thrashing against the coarse sheets, thinking of all those clichés about religious discomfort and trying to spread some body heat down to the foot of bed, where the blankets felt like wet cement across my feet."

"You didn't appreciate the monastic atmosphere, I gather. Nor its neutrality."

"Exactly. The air felt muffled, yet incredibly icy, stripped to bare essentials as if everything that human hands might touch was suspect. It's hard to sleep in a place that has not a scrap of color, not a hint of a cushion or a night-light. One bare bulb surrounded by a globe mounted on the ceiling was all— probably why I gave up trying to read, switched it off and felt my way back to bed, then lay there, staring up into the dark- ness and imagining having to put myself to sleep in such a sensory-deprived place every night. It was pitch dark, a single window high in the wall, coated with a black curtain, I could swear it was black, although now I wonder how far my imagination went, whether it was my expectation of darkness or real darkness that made the room so impenetrable."

"Perhaps the darkness seemed darker because the room was so sparse."

"Whatever, I must have fallen asleep because I woke to a noise, and waking, could make out shapes in the darkness, the door over on the right, the window high on the left, the room vaguely visible. I turned my head on the pillow toward the door, was certain that I saw the handle turning. Usually, in a sleazy hotel, I prop a chair under the doorknob, but in a monastery, where decorum is frozen, eternal? I hadn't thought about intruders, but there was the knob turning, the door cracking open, a cassocked figure entering against the yellow hall light, the door closing again as soundlessly as if it were oiled. And a man in the room."

"A monk?"

"I'm sure. He moved silently, although my ears strained for the swish of his soutane, and I imagined I heard it, then I felt him kneel at the end of the bed. I wanted to hold my breath but thought it would be a sign that I was awake, and so I tried to keep breathing evenly, as if I were relaxed, if not asleep."

"What was he doing? Praying?"

"Possibly."

"What did you do?"

"What could I do? I lay there, he knelt at the end of the bed, and both of us tried to imagine what would happen next. It seemed as if his lips moved, but I couldn't decipher the nature of his prayer."

"Did you speak?"

"No, I lay perfectly still, waiting to hear or see what he would devise. You know, almost welcoming the suspense. Until he rose and stepped up alongside the bed toward my pillow. He moved between the bed and window, blotting out the small edge of light that shone through, and then his hands were around my throat."

Derrick Atman is staring at me, his own hands wrapped around his glass.

"They fit like a collar, and their strength was comforting, even gentle. Except that I could not breathe. I began to thrash and struggle, my body involuntarily rejecting his touch. I'm a strong woman, he had trouble holding on to me like that. I clawed his fingers away from my throat, pushed my hand against his face. He was an inexperienced killer, wasn't prepared for my fingers jabbing at his eyes. He grunted, fell back, while curiously, I kept my supine posture, the blankets now rucked and disheveled around me, but my body laid out as still and straight as before. His breathing came in ragged gasps, but he composed himself, almost as if he were smoothing down his soutane, and then he touched his hand to my head, gently this time, and ran it down the blanket covering the length of my body, along my shoulder, my arm, my belly, my thighs, until he reached my feet, their bump at the end of the bed. As if he were blessing me. Then he turned and slid out of the room as soundlessly as he had entered."

"And what did you do?"

"I went to sleep."

"No way."

"Yes, I slept the creamiest, most luxuriant sleep and might never have believed the night more than a dream except that when I looked into the mirror the next morning, there were faint bruises on my neck."

"Did you say anything?"

"What would I say? I hadn't raised an alarm, hadn't gone running through those corridors calling for help. And I was still alive, even remarkably well."

"Can you explain that?"

"I haven't tried. Perhaps a celibate fetish. He didn't seem dangerous, only strangely compassionate. But weak. He only killed one night, instead of a lifetime."

We sip at our drinks, watch the other patrons in the lounge, the long paneled bar with its buzz of waiters.

"Are you happy?" I ask him.

"Happy?"

"I have this suspicion that men, once they reach forty, are terribly bored with the choices they have made for themselves."

"And?"

"Well, then women become their testing ground, don't they?"

"I'm not testing you on anything."

"But we are in this strange position. Do you usually—?"

"Kill women?"

"Yes."

"Actually, you would be surprised. Men are supposed to be the macho ones, the ones who choose impulsive and violent exits, but many more men than women ask for my assistance."

"Maybe women want female accomplices."

"Did you?"

"No. It seems more appropriate that my—assistant—be a man."

"Do you blame men then, for your restlessness?"

"No, no. They would like to be blamed, but most of the men I've known have been incidental killers."

"Harmless."

"Oh, harmful enough, but unable to translate their desire

for power over life and death into anything much beyond rage. Violent rage, but rarely accurate or effective."

"Ah," he says, nodding. "I understand. Killers but not killers; hatred but not responsibility."

I DROVE THE Dalmatian coast with that type of assassin. It was a wild rocky road that followed the integument of stone and sea with as much jagged determination as he did. That was when I began to think I was capable of being an irredentist for death. He was a journalist tracing a story, snooping out the return of some Cossacks to the Russians by the Allies after the Second World War. Of course, the Russians put them all to death, and he was looking for the bullet holes. He wanted to see blood, although some forty years later, the splashes were pretty much washed away. An irredentist is someone who lives under the suasion and possession of a foreign power, someone who wants to rejoin the state that she feels herself linked to in terms of history and culture. It was a feeling that arose in those territories that had been annexed by the Austro-Hungarians in their urge to compete with empire building against Germany.

By then I wanted to rejoin death, find erasure. There I was with that assassin, who was playing a version of savior, and all I wanted to do was jump into the Adriatic. He was on the other side entirely, enjoying his search for death and dying, and while the sea frothed against the rocks below the road twisting beside the Dalmatian coast, I decided that I was an irredentist for death.

"DID YOU TELL any of your inept killers about your decision?"

"Oh yes, but they didn't hear. They're poor listeners. Most men looking for battles sites are hard of hearing. The gunfire, you know."

"Are they still alive, or do you know?"

"Oh, I'm sure they're avidly alive, still gulping orange juice and wolfing down veal cutlets. Why else seek out murder venues with such grim determination?"

"And so you became an irredentist for death." He is musing, repeating my thoughts as if to taste them.

"Better than other politics. Better than other regions."

"That's bitter. People can't help it if their knuckle bones are turned into relics."

"No, but there's no point encouraging fetishes like that. My own knuckles have done nothing worthy of attention except scrape and gnaw."

I DECIDE IT is my turn to grill him. "Do people often choose to die at night?"

"Mostly. It seems a more private time."

"What's the worst part of your job?"

"Sometimes so many dead people make me sleepy."

That shuts me up.

"So why here?" he asks. "Why a hotel in the very city where you already live?"

"I don't want to make my home a death house. I don't want my friends or Tante Katje to discover me, maybe after days, putrid and rotting. I don't want them to have to take care of the police and coroner and cleanup, the terrible remains of what remains."

"Am I here to spare you or them?"

"Mostly me, I guess. I should admit that."

"But you still want an idyllic setting."

"I've learned that bed and board can never be indiscriminate. I long, when I'm traveling, to find a cozy spot, a good room to retreat to, respite from the slant of foreign rain and the tense charge of tongues that I have to strain to understand. There aren't many old hotels in Calgary."

"Nothing much old at all that I can see."

"Well, it does have age, if you know how to look, if you know where. Easterners claim that this city hasn't grown organically, merely been uncharted, boxes coming out of boxes for a result that's cold and repellent. But there are warm spaces here, if you know how to find them."

"You're defending Calgary again."

"Of course. This is my home base, for years I've come back here, to the fireplace in my condominium, to the stairs that lead to my book-lined bedroom. I live here, I know it's a remorseless city, too adolescent to be compassionate, but it's my version of home, even if it makes me feel homesick."

"Is that why it's good place to die?"

"A perfect place to die. A city refusing to happen, a city that almost disappeared before it appeared, nagged into existence by the Mounted Police and the railway, the joint of the Bow and the Elbow. Brash, snuff-chewing, toe-scuffing Calgary."

"So why are you so eager to leave?"

"That's a question of life, not place. And you're grilling me again. Aren't you supposed to avoid asking your clients why they've engaged you?"

"Does it matter? Who do you think I'd tell?"

He's right, of course. Who could he tell about me?

"You seem to love this city so much," he says. "My experience has been that those who want to die care for nothing, defend nothing, make every space and emotion a void."

"Simple. I want to become a ghost story."

He puts his head down and groans. "You can't be serious."

"Why not? We need more ghosts."

"You're quoting me, my darling."

We're so immersed, my killer and I, that I cannot credit that another voice has spoken, and we turn from the intense posture of our discussion as if dreaming, interrupted by only too plausible a person. A gnomish statue, she's wearing her fur, despite the chinook, and she teeters on the heels of that ridiculous footwear she calls boots.

I gasp, a sudden constriction around my heart. "Tante Katje! What are you doing here?"

"The same thing I could ask you."

"Well, we're having a drink."

"And so was I, over there, by the window. With a friend of mine who needed a sip of alcohol. I saw you come in, but you're not paying attention to the rest of the world."

"I'm sorry—I—"

She nods, then perches on the edge of the third chair without asking if she can stay. "I understand. You discuss important things. You are one of my niece's clients?"

159

"Clients?" Derrick Atman seems as stunned as I am by this apparition. We have been cocooned, so separate that we never thought of interruption. I imagined I had already left.

"Let me introduce you to my aunt. Mr. Atman, this is my Tante Katje, Tante Katje—"

She has already extended her hand, soft with age spots and veins, but still long-fingered, still manicured. She has a streak of vanity, my aunt, although she is as capable of beating a carpet as she is of serving tea. He recovers quickly and rises, bending over her with an unstudied courtliness that makes her smile. She likes men, I realize, and I've never taken a man home to meet her. She has never met my dear one, although once in a while she raises an eyebrow at me and pronounces my color good. That is as close as she comes to telling me that I look like I'm getting laid.

"Would you like a drink with us?"

Behind her, I am shaking my head at him, *no*, but he ignores me, and helps Tante Katje to shed the heavy fur coat, lay its well-oiled pelt across a chair.

"What are you having, *schattebout*?"

"Tea and Benedictine."

"Oh, that sounds good. I'll have the same."

"Are you driving?" I ask.

"Now, stop with the lecture. Of course I'm driving. One little drink of Benedictine won't send me past the speeding limit."

"I wasn't thinking of your speeding."

"They don't plug breathalyzers into little old ladies."

Derrick Atman's face is dimpling, she's delighted him already, and now the two of them will take sides against me, just when I thought I was safe, when my haven was only a few floors away.

"I think they do."

"*Ach*, you. I've never been stopped yet." She turns back to my killer. "Isn't this a nice place? So elegant."

He nods, clearly hoping that he won't give too much away, but she observes him with a quick appraisal that makes my heart sink. Who knows what she'll conclude?

"And I didn't catch your answer. Are you a client of my niece?"

"Yes, actually. She delivers various medical prostheses for us."

"Oh, then you send them all over the world, arms and legs?"

"Yes. They're individually made, so they need to be treated with care." He's clever, has invented something that I might actually do.

"My niece too," says Tante Katje, and I can't quite believe I've heard that, can't imagine what she means. Her English is good, but she sometimes alters the order of sentences so that meanings are disguised. "No, *schattebout*?"

"Yes." I nod at her, then gesture to the waitress, who has reappeared. "What will you have?"

Tante Katje points at me. "Same as what she has."

"Would you like another?" asks Derrick Atman.

"If you will," I say. I want us to be equally drunk; and it seems that we will have to sit through Tante Katje's drink anyway.

"I like to come here," confides Tante Katje when the waitress has moved away. "I imagine you stay in hotels this nice all the time, but I get no chance because I do not travel."

"Have you never been tempted to accompany your niece? She apparently goes everywhere."

"Yes. She has told me that saying she has: 'Good girls go to heaven, but bad girls get to go everywhere else.' But I would be a hindrance, an old lady like me."

"You look very capable of globe-trotting."

"Oh, I am, but I don't want to, you see. I like to stay put here."

"Wouldn't you like to see your family?" He is testing my story against her version.

"It would be a disappointment for all of them. I talk to them on the telephone once a month. That's enough."

"Don't you miss old buildings, European history?"

"Overrated. Most of the old buildings were put to rubble in the war, and there is plenty of history here. Look, the Big Four." She gestures at the photo above the couch where I sit. "They're the history of this town, aren't they, dear?" She addresses the waitress, who is setting down her snifter and teapot, another glass for Derrick Atman.

The waitress looks puzzled.

"Aren't you from Calgary then, dear?"

"Yes, I am."

"Well, the Big Four. The boys who started the Stampede. You should know them!"

"I thought it was just an old picture."

"Oh no, important men, probably responsible for your tips during Stampede."

The waitress shrugs. This goes beyond her job description, she wants to be off the hook. I'm surprised at Tante Katje's enthusiasm, but of course, every year she goes to the Stampede at least four or five times. She's fanatic about the chuck-wagon races.

She grumbles as the waitress walks away. "The young, so unobservant, they don't know their own world." She pours her tea weak, dumps the whole measure of Benedictine into one cup. "Otherwise, a nice bar. Have you stayed in many hotels like this, darling?"

"Quite a few, Tante Katje."

"Don't you prefer these old railway dames better than spanking new ones with glass elevators and open swimming pools?"

I have to chuckle at her, my insouciant aunt, touching up her information about the world. "You're right, Tante. There's a tradition of the umbilical link between railway station and hotel. At the turn of the century, when people alighted from trains, they wanted to be next to a good place to stay."

I don't add my private criterion of how travelers use hotels to escape the responsibilities of family, the toast crumbs of domestic squalor. Hotels are where people eke out honeymoons and anniversaries, where families are rent and mended, where affairs of the heart are secretly conducted. Where a calmly committed murder fits into the decor.

"Yes," says Tante Katje, "I always thought it was important to choose a hotel with a face like a dowager, an ample derrière, upholstered. New hotels are too blank for me, shiny glass and metal, no personality. I want the chairs worn down a little, rubbed, the nap flattened toward the stuffing. Like here, from people settling with a drink, crossing their legs and leaning back. That's the sign of a good hotel."

She's described the attitude of waiting I cherish so much, the seduction of graceful rooms, oversized, eloquent in their desire to accompany. I do like to sit in a luminous place, not dilated with light, but shaded as if to lull. The new is too new, too cold, without a touch of fusty comfort.

"But still, things have changed a little too much. Hotels used to have tables to read newspapers, deep chairs beside shaded lamps, ferns beside brocade-curtained windows."

She has her own version of refinement, and it touches me. I owe her at least one story.

"You know, Tante Katje, two weeks ago, in Brussels, I stayed in the Metropole."

"The Metropole! You stayed there? You didn't tell me. Now, that was the famous place before the war; all the fashionable people went there."

"Yes, and it's still incredible. The walls are encrusted with Tunisian marble, even the ceilings are gilded, and every column is carved marble. There are leather banquettes everywhere, old and cracked, but deep, and a gallery of wrought iron chandeliers."

"Ahhh, you lucky girl."

She's delighted with what she thinks is my good fortune, although staying there, I felt muffled in a crenellated museum, too much gilt for gilt, the walls bloated with faded importance. And the nineteenth-century excess, more palace than twentieth-century hotel, time missing interpretation. What I recall most vividly now was a man with an overpainted escort in the brasserie, everything about him exact, the precision of his fork on his plate, the sharp creases of his knotted tie. It was clear he had purchased the woman's company, she was a diversion from his graphite life, a quick fuck that he would leave there amidst the elderly women clutching the saddles of their purses, the waiters legging their work behind long white aprons, while the mirrors wavered marble explications around them.

It was an archaic place to have a glass of wine and a sandwich, but I sat on a tapestried chair and watched the etched glass over the door and the potted plants that clustered the corners, suddenly homesick for the dearth of such palms in Canada, the dearth of coatracks in our restaurants, the dearth of wrought iron chandeliers, the dearth of riveted leather chairs holding out their arms in front of grave fireplaces, all those attempts to collate history's singular failures.

Although there is never a dearth of assassins, eager to buy a woman's eyebrows and fingernail polish.

I knew that the Metropole would be a superb place to die, among the lingering smoke of ancient cigarettes, the brave suspenders of aging waiters, figures bent with plates and expectation, waiting for time to contract. But how to conclude such a conclusion? I had brought no sleeping pills, hadn't even brought along a razor. Either method required a self-reliance that I couldn't count on. And a mess.

And then, riding the Edoux lift the second morning, descending to the French Renaissance foyer, I recognized the solution. I could hang myself from one of the wrought iron curlicues of the lift bars, the lift I rode up and down with an attendant to lower the steel cage door, to clang it open. As if I were in a Bertolucci movie. I even tested the possibility. The second morning I took a silk scarf and knotted it to the outer rank of steel to see if the motion of the lift would have sufficient strength. It did; the scarf tore in half. But then I began to worry about there being enough time to truly lose my breath, whether I wouldn't be rescued too quickly. The hotel management didn't like guests riding the *ascenseur* without the attendant. They were afraid we would damage the Edoux lift.

But in that Edoux lift, knowing that I would need an accomplice, knotting my scarf around the cold metal of an elaborately art deco rank of bars, I discovered in myself a homesickness to die in Canada, despite the Brussels trees leafing into a winter green slow as light, despite the lugubrious perfection of the Metropole. The Edoux lift sighed with languid suggestion, and I knew then and there, standing in its open shaft, that I would go back to Calgary, I would say my good-byes, I would hire a suitable killer and I would assist at my own execution. I would do this immediately, accomplish my irredentist task within a couple of weeks.

"You know," Tante Katje is proud of her European pedigree, even if she won't set foot on the continent again, "Sarah

Bernhardt, Isadora Duncan—they all stayed there. Goering, the Sovay Council, Einstein, Madame Curie."

"What a mixture!" Derrick Atman exclaims.

"That's old Europe for you. And people wonder why I won't go back. Murderers dining with actresses everywhere. You should have seen the Amstel in Amsterdam during the war. Full of Nazis."

I've stayed in so many of those decaying places with flocked fleur-de-lis wallpaper and fringed cassocks crouching like docile dogs at the foot of uncomfortable chairs. Thick carpets, horsehair furniture, dusty chandeliers. Columns and more columns, as if they actually help to hold up the obligatory lobbies and ballrooms. Mirrors whose frames bespeak entire dynasties and framed portraits of long-dead aristocrats perfectly willing to terminate heiresses. Hotels harbor lovers and financial secrets even while they succumb to display. Their baroque enclosures promise an exit to another world, connective tissue for extinction, erasure of the self's facts. Staying in a palace hotel is no time to be on a budget. Those are places where it is de rigueur to order a glass of ice wine, an extra snifter of brandy, that eloquent basket of breadsticks.

"I think we should revive billiard rooms," says Derrick Atman, "but those romantic emporiums of cigars and portly bellies have been overtaken by lank-legged young men who aim pool cues through the hair that falls into their eyes."

"And women," Tante Katje agrees. How does she know?

"You know," I say, "in the old days, ninety percent of room service calls were for bellboys to bring ice water to the rooms. Ice water was the luxury. That accounts for the persistent presence of the lowly ice bucket."

"How do you know this?" my killer asks me. We are all confirming one another's knowledge, as if that will provide accountability.

"Traveling. Sometimes in the dead of night, when I can't sleep, I read the literature lying around, hotel promotions, descriptions of sister establishments, and I find these odd statistics tucked between proclamations of how comfortable the beds are, how elegant the draperies." I don't add that I walk the halls, checking stairways, following the scent of perfume or a cigar. "And did you know that a morning newspaper means that they've cut an inch off the bottom of the door?"

Tante Katje picks up my play. She always does, and I realize that is why we never fought, never had a serious head-to-head. Again I wince at her generous care, her determination not to overmother me, make me her daughter.

She giggles. "Did you know that Statler used to lie in the bathtub of each room to see what the guest would see from that position? Can you imagine? And he was a famous hotelier."

"You knew him personally, Tante Katje?"

"Of course not. And César Ritz suffered a nervous breakdown from all those years of wandering the corridors of his hotels, checklist in hand, writing down the things that needed to be done. Repairing worn carpet, loose doorknobs, putting up sheerer curtains, repainting walls. It drove the poor man crazy."

"Where did you find that out?" asks Derrick Atman.

"Oh, I read hotel stories too. Very interesting, these people who want the world under their roof. Most hoteliers are gamblers and drinkers. It's the liquor in the lounge, those games in card rooms."

"Now," I interrupt, "they just provide a bed, with posted room rates, reading lamps, clock radios and telephones." But I know what she's saying. Everything is available in a hotel. Crested stationery should I choose to write a note, a beautifully appointed bed, a good bedside light, a television with an infinite number of channels if I should decide that the world is not quite so banal as I thought, if I need to remind myself of good reasons to abandon it.

A hotel is where an ordinary person can pretend, despite the small humiliations of the oblivious world, that she can presume to have servants. A bellboy, a chambermaid, a pantryman somewhere making sugar roses, room service—all the trappings without having to hire servants or account for them, without having to do much more than pick up the phone and offer a tip. And everything else as well, a supply of food and drink, the pleasures of table, rest for the exhausted and titillation for the bored, those surfeit with experience. Staying in a hotel offers a set ritual of exchange, always predictable, always present. But a home away from home? Never. A hotel is not a home but a place to fantasize, to stare into reflecting pools, browse atriums, ride elevators to floors full of boxlike rooms harboring other strangers.

"Don't you ever wonder," asks Tante Katje, "who teaches the chambermaids to make the beds the way they do?"

I can't imagine her staying in a hotel, but she demonstrates such finesse with details that I realize she must have at sometime.

She's in full flight. "And who decided how a hotel should run? It needs barbers, bellboys, cooks, chambermaids, waiters. A bar and a restaurant, a beauty salon and a gift shop."

I think of the warmed room upstairs—the lights on, the television scrolling information, the curtains drawn and the bed turned down. I am suddenly powerfully sleepy.

But Tante Katje won't stop, and Derrick Atman is giving her his undivided attention. "There's a blocked-off tunnel in the basement that leads to the train station, you know. The bellhops used to meet the train and wheel the luggage through it while the guests went on aboveground. That was when bellhops were hired for good deportment, when call boys marched through the lobby waving important messages in white-gloved hands. And there were regulations for ice — it had to be broken into one-inch square pieces. Can you imagine all the rules for employees, the service manuals, the stern hands of chefs, and the noses of stewards, the waiters who turned a blind eye to guests slipping whiskey into their ginger ale during prohibition? This lounge has License Number 1 from the Alberta Liquor Control Board, but it was a men's-only bar until 1970."

My aunt must have grilled some sighing waitress slogging a tall pot of coffee in the Rimrock. She is pickpocketing my carefully planned death, a quick-fingered thief, magpie eager. And then, as unexpectedly as she appeared, she stops herself, deftly extracts a ten dollar bill from her purse and puts it on the table.

"But now," she says, "I've talked enough, and I must defy the police that you are so certain will breathalyze me. Goodnight *schattebout*, and goodnight to you too." She stands, make a brief incline toward Derrick Atman and reaches for the glossy pelt of her coat.

He helps her slide her arms into the sleeves, fumbling a bit. I realize he is tired, and I wonder if he is too tired to proceed, if, under the bandage, his hand throbs.

"Thank you so much," says Tante Katje, "and you should take that hand to bed soon. Goodnight dearest, and sweet dreams." She bends to kiss me and whispers, "He's very nice, but don't keep him too long." Then she is stepping away, her body a lively raccoon. At the door to the lobby, knowing we're watching, she turns and blows us a kiss, then disappears.

"Excuse me," I say to my companion. "I'm going to find the women's room."

I hurry, and around the corner where the bellhop keeps his

desk, see Tante Katje just heading out the front door. "Tante Katje!"

She appears not to hear me, is conferring with the doorman, who laughs at some quip she has made.

I call again, "Tante Katje," and push through the revolving door after her.

She turns, raises her brows. "Have I forgotten something?"

"I—no, I just wanted to say goodnight and thank you."

"Oh, I left the bill with you, dear. I think that nice man can buy an old lady a drink. Oh no, I forgot, I did leave a *tientje*." She winks. "Be careful. He looks married."

I nod. "All right. And don't worry, I'm fine. Perhaps you should stay in a hotel, Tante. Not now, but someday. For just one night."

She smiles and pats my arm; then she is gone, stepping down the windy street as daintily as if she were on a catwalk. Well.

No one wants dying to be a bureaucratic adagio, but she convinces me again that it is better for me to conclude here, on neutral ground, than in my home. She'll know immediately what I've done, and what's more, I believe she'll understand, even be glad of that final drink, that unconsummated good-bye.

‿◦

HERE IS MY pilgrimage resumed. Travelers learn to look at ceilings, at floors, learn to examine the artifacts that they might have missed, the significance of arrival and departure. Heels click across the lobby in a ghostly echo. Is this the last space I will cross, will my footsteps be burned in some way into this marble floor?

An earlier assassin and I spent a night here long, long ago. I lay awake crying, but I was saved by a fire alarm, which turned out to be a real fire, some old wiring in the Marquis Room. I was young. I didn't know he was an assassin, and I didn't know that I'd been saved by a hair, by the old hotel groaning under the weight of its need for renovation and rewiring. I understand only now, having had so many years to assess assassins. So it seems fitting that I should return to this hotel, to a room where I know I will be saved by assassination rather than from it.

⌒

I DO GO to the women's room, close myself in a stall and sit down, prop my chin on my hands. Public toilets in hotels are strangely benign, devoid of advertising or the piquancy of graffiti. They pretend to be powder rooms rather than toilets, cures rather than infections.

I feel like flannel, exhausted, unable to think clearly. I remember times when I've gotten the last bed in a city over-flowing with conventions or festivals. The very last bed, so grimy that I should have cringed but was instead extravagantly grateful that I had managed to find a bed at all. That is how I feel now, as if I could sleep forever.

There is the sound of heels, a toilet stall door slamming and a woman's voice, "Shit," as she slides the latch closed. Must have caught her finger.

I crouch on my own throne, listening. She rustles and undresses, pees loudly and flushes twice. I wait—I need to face the row of mirrors alone—until, by the silence in the room, it seems she has left.

But when I swing open the stall door, she is leaning against the bank of sinks with her arms crossed, her leather coat and tall boots making her look like a version of Nancy Sinatra, but more beautiful, her russet hair careless around her face.

I stop, her attitude demands that I stop. Surely she cannot know that I've been watching her across the Chicago E, that I've been surveying her restlessness with my own.

"I've been watching you," she says.

Is this a confession, an accusation? A trick?

"I've been watching you," she says again. "Our rooms face each other, on the fifth floor, and I can see you."

"I can see you too. " I say this quietly, almost in a whisper.

"But there's nothing to see with me. While you, you unpack and pack and unpack again, you pace, you lie on the bed, then jump up, you pace around the room, you cry, you argue with that man, you change your clothes. Is he trying to persuade you to do something you'd rather not?"

"No. He's a friend. He's helping me."

"You were at dinner for a terribly long time, arguing, even crying again."

"How—?"

"I followed you—easy. You're oblivious. I sat in the back of Divino's and you didn't even notice. Then I followed you to the river, to Prince's Island and back."

"Why?"

"I worry about women I see through windows. Especially if they don't pull their curtains. A woman who closes her curtains is secure."

"But I'm fine. There's nothing to worry about."

"No, you have a restless light around you, sometimes green, sometimes indigo. I could see your anxiety the moment I looked out of my window across to yours. You're about to undertake something you fear, you're about to jump."

She's aggressive, but there is a nervous tenderness in her eyes, around her mouth. Imagine that, I think, an antiassassin for my perfect assassin. What strange coincidences, what accidents of reprieve are stumbling across my path.

"What were you writing?" I ask, daring to brush past her, to turn on the taps and put my hands under the water.

"A note to you. I slid it under your door."

"I didn't find it. You had the wrong door."

"No, right door, right door. You probably didn't notice. It's there."

"Well," I dry my hands on a rough crumple of paper towels, "you needn't be concerned. "I'm having a wonderful time, a perfect time. Just tired, that's all."

She doesn't speak again, but looks directly at me, taking in my eyes, my mouth, the very tilt of my ears.

"Thanks for your concern." I move to walk around her to the door, but she catches my arm roughly, holds me there. I don't try to pull away but stand, docile, waiting.

"There's no sin to restlessness," she says. "We all have it. We learn to live with it."

And without letting go of my arm, she pulls me closer and kisses me full on the mouth, her lips as soft as the leaves of a clover, her breath smelling of mint, her skin against mine impossibly smooth.

I kiss her back.

STARING UP AT a Victorian arcade in Leeds, where I had gone to deliver a mysterious tin box, I stumbled and fell, tripping on the uneven paving stones. One quick stagger and I crashed to my knees in terrible supplication, while two Yorkshire housewives rushed to my side and pecked at me, hauling me to my feet as if standing upright would ease my scraped skin.

"Are you all right then, luv?"

"Dear, dear, those paving stones is uneven."

"Yes," I answered huskily, "I'm fine."

I was on the verge of tears, not for my bloodied knees but their kindness, the touch of their work-worn hands on my arms. Their string handbags bounced over their wrists, but even busy with market-day provisioning, they took time to be shocked at my fall, knowing that they too could crumple to the ground without notice.

That was when I understood. My dear one can pick me up, but I will always fall again.

DERRICK ATMAN IS waiting under the black and white pose of the Big Four, turning the empty glass in his unbandaged hand.

I'm glad to see him. The woman has made his resurrection crystal clear, and now I'm eager to conclude our bargain.

"Let's go," I say. "Let's go to bed."

"Are you really sure?" he asks. "You know you can change your mind."

"Enough talking. I'm sure. You're the solution."

"You said you wanted a gentle killer."

"Doesn't everybody?"

"Well, people think they prefer someone gentle. But there are those who like the drama of a brutal death, the marks of guns or knives as testimony. It depends."

"But—"

"I'm just letting you know that asking for a gentle killer is a contradiction in terms."

"An oxymoron?"

"Exactly. A killer cannot be expected to be outstandingly gentle or he would choose another profession."

"But you seem gentle, trustworthy." I'm puzzled. What is he trying to tell me?

He nods. "I do my best. But I have my professional side."

He stands, retrieves my coat and then his. I fumble for money, as if I have already forgotten the requirements of trans-action. The hotel bill. Who will pay the bill? My expense account is closed. He will, of course, Derrick Atman, part of the service he offers, the account settled with neatness and dis-patch, no loose ends, although he must have nerves of steel. The bill leaves evidence behind, more clues that can be traced to him, despite his gloves, despite his respectable demeanor.

"I've already paid," he says. "Your aunt left a ten."

We move toward the alcove of elevators, their genteel brass surround. Shades of Tante Katje. I'm nervous. "Did you know," I say, evoking her arch voice, "that there used to be a lounge on the top floor of the hotel, but respectable women wouldn't go there because it would appear they were going to someone's room."

Derrick Atman laughs. "We are going to a room, and we're respectable."

THERE ARE, THE despairing know, two dimensions and two palettes, time and space, both dynamic, but frequently invisible to each other, mysterious energies that take no account of human interference, ignoring inquisitive and acquisitive gestures. And so we who despair travel to the world we expect to find, and taking our time with us—the interminable wristwatch, the ubiquitous travel alarm—find exactly what we expect. Or find instead white nights, the sun rotating a landscape of its own, chronometric challenges insisting again that the traveler is out of time and tune, lost to hours and seconds, hoist on a minute hand, time something that we wish to forget and cannot, its tyranny keeping us ruddered to the apron strings of gravity.

WE ARE IN the Palliser Hotel, my killer and I, a grand CPR hotel in the old style, full of chandeliers and pillars and staircases that float toward heaven.

This hotel has a history; peculiar secrets and ghosts drift the softly padded halls, hover above the lowered voices of the staff. On the floor above the mezzanine persistent footsteps pace, and the rooms sometimes waft cold drafts. The lions shouldering the musicians' gallery have yawned sadly for almost eighty years. Communities are judged by the quality of their hotels. Workmen died building this hotel, and Palliser was a man who thought the prairies a wasteland. He argued that nothing could grow here, all would surely perish.

If any building contradicts raw Calgary, it has to be the Palliser, with its Chicago-style straight geometric lines, the E-shape so that all rooms have outside light, the repeated mahogany doors to the guest rooms, the postered brass beds, the windows that open to let in the wind. An Edwardian hotel, the brick bread oven in the subterranean kitchen glowing a bright heat that never dies.

Anachronistic, most would say, although now, in this antihistorical age, we crave anachronism, find it quaint and inspiring. This is the kind of hotel where people want to get married, where tea dances and stock deals take place side by side. These plastered plinths witness visits from ambassadors and conferences of comb salesmen, official delegations of cattle breeding. Like its cousins, this hotel has become a wax museum, but rather than strolling through, looking, the guest is permitted for the briefest time to imagine him or herself belonging to a gracious well-heeled era, far from the roar of aggressive traffic, the nasty invective of polluted streets, the holler of billboards selling cablevision and naked perfumes. The crumbling decay is as important to the gilt decor as the newly terrazzoed floors, the manners of the top-hatted door-men dressed as if they were in Edward's reign.

Everything conspires toward this drama. My desire to die, my gentle accomplice, my resilient double. For such theater, a revolving door at the entrance is essential, the sweep of rubber along the edging announcing a visitor trapped for a brief moment in a glass cage. To enter, one must spin oneself through a version of puzzle, a compartmented circle, tempting to the coattails and eager to trap the unwary.

The drama continues to unfold under a restless composi-tion of chandeliers, a grand curved staircase, gleaming wood, and in the dining room, tooled leather wall panels, the fireplace lit only on the coldest days, but there to suggest potential comfort. Columns flute their way toward the higher-than-high ceilings, the possibility of fans and ceiling moths, tapestries and marble cornices. Here is occasion for monument, a pile of stone, a reliquary.

Every railway station catering to restlessness requires an attached hotel. That is the guiding principle behind the construction of the Palliser. Every room provides ingenious appliances, ironing board, hair dryer, warming pipes, padded hangers. To be fair, the decoration has resisted excess, not too much flocked wallpaper, instead, a cool green aura and tiles the color of salmon skin.

I tested other places. The Frankfurterhof, once approached through an arcaded garden court, now a closed-in conservatory, the elegant fountain in front reduced to a traffic island, the windows under their eyebrows surprised. It was too sad. When I arrived at the side door, a limp-haired and green-sick doorman did not want to heft my bags. Nor could I succumb to the Imperial Palace in Nice, shabby and frayed, the white-coated waiter hustling in with coffee and croissants every morning, no matter that I lay naked in bed.

All a person wants is the private act of a key, the commonplace of new soap next to thickly folded towels. We all—tourists, conference delegates, government officials, business travelers, job seekers, awkward friends, long-lost brothers, rock stars, married people having affairs and not least, potential suicides—want the same thing. A neutral space.

So the hotel becomes it own suggestion, a place for passion to erupt, for power to be brokered, for strangers to meet, life in a capsule, trays producing food without the jam stains and smell of burning in the kitchen at home, deference purchased, the subtle frictions of the external world softened or erased. Amidst the amenities of eiderdown comforters, terry cloth bathrobes, scented soap and shampoo, name-brand bottled water, shower caps, chocolates on the pillow at night, fruit baskets, bathroom scales, heated towel racks, turn-down service, the *clefs d'or* of attended needs, death can be engaged.

In short, a theater, with the guest starring in her own drama. And here is mine. I am going to ride up to my room with my killer. Despite the ghost of Robert Barr, killed by this same descending elevator cage, I will enter the lift, ready for my rising curtain.

THE ELEVATOR DOORS stumble open, and there stands my woman, in the corner of that small room, her face flushed with the hour's remains.

"Going up?" she asks.

Derrick Atman doesn't flinch, although I am sure that he recognizes her. "Five," he says. "You've already pushed it."

She nods, fixes her eyes on me, a relentless stare that will not barter time, while the elevator doors close.

I THINK OF the rituals of hotels, the language of hospitality. Walk-ins, reservations, no-shows, under-stays, check-outs, arrivals, departures. I used to be one of those people hotels hate. Not the kind who make a reservation and then don't appear, the no-shows. No, I'm a perennial under-stay, booked for two days and staying one, booked for three days and staying two, unwilling to still my own restless feet. It's foolish, of course, because the extra night is almost always paid for, and when I leave a hotel, I put myself at the mercy of my bank account. But my restlessness wins. I want to try another place, a different set of elevators, a different barman's wrist action on the cocktail shaker. I'm the reason hotels overbook.

I don't expect a canopied bed. A plain mattress afloat with a duvet is enough, a padded headboard, pillows that mold to the body, a window that opens. Once I'm through the door I'll slip on this sleeve of comfort and hidingness, the stage of my last few breaths. The story goes that when a person steps into an elevator, sad spirits are lifted. Will Robert Barr's spirit lift mine? And do I want my sadness stayed? Do I want to send my friendly accomplice on his way without concluding his business?

Hotels set out to make their guests feel at home, but argue for a short stay rather than a lifetime. I've tried them all. Hotels in Berlin frown. Hotels in Vienna coruscate. Hotels in London camp, as if trying to impress Dickens, as if the nineteenth century will double back in its tracks. But this hotel, in the wild west, Calgary, Canada, is discrete, even gentle, despite its gatherings of salesmen and cattle sellers, the newly well off mixed with those set in their ways. Anyone can check in, ask for anything. A bouquet of California heather, an Egyptian cigar, an extra bath towel, a dish of almonds, every whim invented by the dirge of last enjoyments. Including hot and cold killers and their antidotes.

The concierge with the crossed keys at his lapel is meant to fulfill requests, cross-reference the postal clerk moonlighting as waiter, the taxi driver who spends his evenings concocting drinks in the bar. Hotel employees have always been a comfort, reminding me that I am not the only one who performs deliveries. They sift the strange music of names, walk down corridor after corridor, one room jigsawed to the next.

And hotels harbor nightclubs, ballrooms, offices, laundry and valet rooms, barber and beauty shops, telephone rooms, refrigeration rooms, incineration rooms, boiler rooms, all beyond the guest rooms circulating people, one with twin beds, a suite with king-size, an ordinary double, mattress firmness regular or extra, mattress size six feet across and seven feet long, platformed, the sandbox design cheek by jowl with the occasional roller cot. And security—does the door lock, can the windows be jimmied? An electronic card supersedes the metal key, the small personal safe, the peephole, the Do Not Disturb sign.

I'm adding these details up, running through the tally as if to keep this woman's eyes from seeing too much of what I want.

THIS MUST BE the slowest elevator I have ever entered, and I can't stop myself from quoting *Dog Sleeps*, the book resting in my suitcase. "'Last night, out walking, I saw a hotel burning.'"

"A burning hotel," she says. "A good dream. They should suffer periodic burning, hotels, although we're snobbish enough to want to stay in these old ones with marble floors and blue-blooded staircases. Of course, we expect the amenities of a new hotel, bathrooms functional as textbooks, with regulated showers and a tub long enough to stretch out in. The contradictions of temporary accommodation. Once we've fisted the key, the room is *ours*, not a neutral space we've purchased for a few hours."

Derrick Atman and I both stare at her, but she continues, as if this soliloquy were planned, rehearsed. As if we are a paying audience.

"Well, a body has to lodge somewhere, and hotels are preferable to the discomfort of an inquisitorial visit to an acquaintance. My friends ensure that their guest rooms are dank, with quilts that slide away during the night. Their bathroom floors are uncommonly cold, their shutters rattle interminably. Staying with friends is either a cure for friendship or an act of piety, and, I tell you, it is best for all concerned if you never succumb to the informative voyeurism of discovering the prophylactics in the medicine cabinet, testing the shampoo on the tub ledge or searching through the drawer where the cutlery is nestled."

"I suppose *you* are an ideal guest," says Derrick Atman dryly.

"No, I change my stripes depending on the circumstances. The quiet guest can be ominous, sending host or hostess into voluble arias of things to do and see, a tour guide's crucible. The voluble guest, the one who gets up at seven to wake everyone who wishes to linger over morning, is even worse, causing host or hostess to wish them abed, insist that they ought to try to sleep in, read a book or go for a protracted stroll through the neighborhood's back lanes. I can be any of those. I do as I please."

She must have stumbled on a reference book for incipient travelers, those who cherish irrepressible movement, as if destination were Ariadne's thread, as if destination were possible. I will the elevator to move, the hydraulic counterweights to hurry, but she can't be stopped.

"Staying with friends, faint or fair, is dubious, although some travelers swear by it, claim the insider track is the quickest way to the nerve center of a place, shown the sites and sights *en famille* as it were, rather than *carte blanche*. But I hate having to put up with cute children, how they will play 'Chopsticks' at six in the morning and put lollipops in your hair. How their parents are disappointed if there is nothing to apologize for."

"I can't imagine," says Derrick Atman, "why anyone would do that to you." His dislike for the woman is visible, transparent as wind.

She ignores him. "Now, staying in a small hotel, the pension, the bed and breakfast, that cozy arrangement, is also fraught. One is apt to be asked a range of questions, apt to be identified, searched out, subjected to inquisitions of history and destination that are uncomfortable if one is traveling with a companion less than documentable but more than celibate. Motels are the solution to that, the western variety, No Tell, check-in anonymous, pay and escape. The mattress will sport a plastic cover, like the soap and the glasses, and the television is likely bolted down, but you can't beat a motel for anonymity, for the bum's rush. And tour hotels—with their impersonal maids and terrible phone lines, their gray and huddled mattresses that have seen so many sad mistakes—are no alternative. The rank smell of disinfectant hangs in the corridors, and those corridors of endless rooms are cursed by Kafka."

"So what do you recommend?" Derrick Atman wants to test her. I can see that she strains his patience, and he has been until now a very patient man.

"A medium-sized hotel that refuses to be part of a chain but is still large enough to ignore its guests. Large enough to cash travelers' cheques but small enough that the hallways do not creak with footsteps; large enough to have a lift but no higher than five stories; with maids who smile but who do not smile knowingly, having memorized the wrinkles in the sheets or the shape of your graying underwear left drying on the shower rack. These are the places where voyeurism can be practiced discreetly and where the tourist and the openly avaricious traveler alike can cling to a modicum of inside knowledge, can pretend that the people at breakfast, that strange ritual of eating the first meal of the day in a large mutual room with others rattling their newspapers and spooning their hard-boiled eggs, are not merely fellow tourists but citizens staying in town on business or even pleasure. An insider's choice."

This is the longest elevator ride I have ever taken.

The woman and my kindly killer are battling over something, but I cannot imagine what or why. They do not know one another, they are strangers.

And I am so tired, so tired.

WHY IS THIS elevator taking so long? The woman is standing in front of the door, telling hotel stories, her hands gesturing detail.

Derrick Atman is pulling on his gloves.

WHEN WE REACH five, the elevator bell will ping before the doors slide open.

"Five," the woman will say. "Our stop." But she won't stop talking. "You see," she'll say, "how easy it is to sound like a tour guide, a travel agent, a guidebook, an authority. You see how tempting it is to become the lead character in Anne Tyler's *Accidental Tourist*, complete with a compilation of restaurants and their side dishes, architecture's solemnities, the nose-smeared windows of bus excursions."

We'll leave the elevator with her, but take the first corridor while she proceeds to the next wing, where she will enter that room facing ours, where she will again light her square of window. Where she will wait.

"Goodnight," Derrick Atman will call after her. And is it my imagination, or will there be a seam of finality in his voice?

"Goodnight," she'll call, already down the corridor. "Happy hunting. And remember, I'm watching you."

"Good-bye," I'll say softly, watching the float of her auburn hair, her long stride. "Good-bye."

She'll get along, she'll find a way to make do. Tomorrow morning she'll wake, stare at our drawn curtains, our window still open a crack. She'll hesitate, then throw her clothes into her bag and take a cab to the airport, on to the next hotel, to another delivery, another imaginary city.

⁓

MY CAREFULLY CHOSEN assassin will unlock the door to our room, and we'll step inside with as much slow courtesy as if we have not been around the world together. Far below, there will rise the rush and grind of a morning freight train—how can it be so early so late?—on the tracks behind the hotel, its horn pulling through the town's slowed streets, its cars heavy with wheat and wood and wind.

Derrick Atman will hang the Do Not Disturb sign out, then close the door and click the dead bolt home.

"You know," I'll say, "in Spain, the Do Not Disturb sign says, *No Molesten*. 'Don't molest.'"

Perhaps he'll tell me a riddle about how my expectations have too much to do with trains, hotels, restaurants, museums, cities and their sights. Perhaps he'll unfold for me a map of travel's shadow plot.

Derrick Atman will bend to pull off his shoes, and with his gloved fingers pick up a crisp piece of folded paper that's lying on the floor by the door.

"That must be the note she said she'd left," I'll say, holding out my hand.

"No," he'll say. "It's for me."

I'll insist. "She said she'd left a note for me. Give it here."

He'll hesitate, narrow his eyes, then shrug and pass the note, which I'll unfold, my fingers slow and clumsy.

When he reads this, he'll kill you. Be careful.

I'll shake my head. Of course. That's what I want him to do. Why does she think she needs to warn me?

I'll hold that paper between my fingers, and yes, I'll read the echo of my earlier note, the letter I mailed my dear one. *When you read this, you'll kill me. Be careful not to hate me, please.*

I'll toss her note on the television console, next to the surprising flower arrangement, then go into the bathroom, pee and brush my teeth without bothering to shut the door. I know this Derrick Atman well enough now.

He'll keep talking, as if the woman's meditation on hotels is spooling over and over. "If I hadn't put the sign out, she'd be in here giving us a lecture on this hotel, why it seems warm in this room, how the pillows are inviting rather than slabs of foam. Here's a ceiling a person can stare up at." And he'll flop down on the bed, put his gloved hands behind his head and stare at the ceiling.

I won't be listening. I'll pull my hair back and wash my face, touch cool water to my forehead. Think of the chinook

sifting frost from shirred trees. I'll think about buying maps.
I buy them even if I will never open their corrugated flaps to
try to orient myself within some enigmatic pattern of streets.
In various rooms that I rent or visit, the maps unfold across
my bed, and I do not bother to remove them when I can
bring myself to crawl between the sheets or under the covers.
While I search for sleep, they spill their tenacious names
across a web of lines. I bring them home with me to Calgary,
shove them into a bookcase that bulges with plans of distant
cities, countries, islands. They suggest that I will be able to
find myself, to discover a destination. So far they have not
helped at all. But here I am.

He will be rambling on, talking as if to himself. "No, this
hotel is experienced. It is possible to die here because death
has happened here before."

I'll hear that and sing out, "And your goal is to ensure
that."

"Exactly. I am required to do what you tell me to do."

I'll laugh. He's so unlike the other assassins, their clumsy
good intentions, their terrible lack of finesse.

When I come out of the bathroom, he'll be holding her
note in his bandaged hand, which I'm accustomed to now, the
white gauze against his warm skin, the gloves off, hidden
somewhere, in his pocket perhaps.

Across the way the red-headed woman will stand in the
frame of her window, hands on hips, staring at us. "Do you
think," I'll ask, "she's the ghost of someone who killed herself
here?"

"Do you know her?" he'll ask.

"No, but she seems familiar."

I'll look across at her and wave.

She'll wave back, then begin to undress, slowly, unzipping
and unbuttoning with a stripper's seduction.

187

"We're obliging them," I'll speculate, the towel in my hand, watching her step out of her skirt, slide off the same pantyhose I watched her don, peel down to elegant lace underwear, "dying here so we can haunt the place, provide the building with a little éclat. Every good hotel needs a ghost flitting through the lobby and the assembly rooms, a cool breeze drifting between the corporeal and the spirit world."

And without turning, I will feel him standing behind me. He will move silent as vapor, watching her too, but sharply.

"Enough then," Derrick Atman will say and snap the curtains closed. "Enough. Does this room suit you? Are you comfortable here? You'll be treated like a person, whatever the medical examiner deduces, you'll be handled gently."

"It's a good room," I'll say, before I collapse to the edge of the bed.

⌒

I WON'T TELL him, but I have been shocked by rooms, the room in New York that hadn't been cleaned, curtains torn down and tied to the bedposts, three half-empty bottles of champagne lolling their open necks on bed stand and dresser, the covers rucked on the floor and the sheets crumpled with stain, the pillows tortured into bolsters. I missed the occupants by a few seconds. They must have been the tidy couple descending in the elevator, their elbows tucked against their ribs as if to contain the pleasure they had bartered. Smelling their lingering breath, I wanted to faint into the stained and still-warm bed sheets, the rucked covers taunting my aloneness, my very appointment with homesickness.

Traveling has become my version of self-punishment.

I ache with grief, I relive my angry losses. I travel to avoid forgiving myself. To avoid my dear one, who would love me back to life.

My dear one. I asked him to kill me, but he refused.

My dear one, whom I leave. But gently.

I'll stretch out on the bed and sigh. I'm tired. He's kept me talking.

And Derrick Atman, my carefully chosen killer, will sit at my feet, will take my right foot in his hand, pull off my thin cotton sock, and begin to rub the sole, his thumbs working the arch, down over the heel and up to the ball of my foot, his fingers pressing my toes as if to semaphore some message.

I'll stretch and groan.

And he'll say nothing, his hands persistent as his listening has been all night, his strange transcendence of the deafness gene that marks clumsy assassins.

"Mmmm, that's wonderful," I'll whisper. "I've been traveling so long I'm footsore."

"Shhhhh."

"But your hand," I'll murmur. "Doesn't that hurt your hand?"

"Shhhhh."

Through my feet will tingle the slow thickening of the desire my dear one has gifted me, a languid spill that could resemble the climb of light at dawn, the parting of a soft mouth, the wide-flung turn of a knee.

There is no similarity between sex and death.

～◯

WHY IS EVERY killer convinced that his or her method is original, a complete invention, treading a path where no sneaker has ever gone, a route undiscovered? Of course, the paths of lovers and killers are remarkably alike, a track migrated into the ground, bearing the weight of many feet, a veritable ant trail complete with markings and their cynicisms.

Where will the ambiguous desires of love and travel mesh? Can either be stopped or started? When is travel a pleasure, and when is it torture? Can movement peel open the parable of a layered blood orange? Love is travel's loss, a jolt of map-lessness, the iconic jest of experience made hollow. Not even the echo of an Alhambra can fill that space.

～◯

I WILL LIE entranced on that bed and refuse to think of answers or questions. I will thumb my next plane ticket, imagine a tram that can carry me back to the nineteenth century, invent an itinerary impossible to follow, pack a suitcase full of maps of disappeared places.

My worst destinations were assassins hungry for departure, whispering a secret mantra to detour any trip resembling love.

Go away.

I WILL ARRIVE at last. I will step into new places eagerly, strain my ears to decipher a newly heard language. Perhaps my pyramid mystic was prescient, and the perfect destination will deafen me.

GUIDEBOOKS. DERRICK ATMAN will lend me a guidebook. I've tried to use guidebooks to find a home for myself, to uncover a place where I can settle, let my bones relax like this, allow my feet to emerge from their walking shoes. But guidebooks are too clever by half, too determined to paint their subjects in sleazy neon, to argue excitement on the basis of night life.

There ought to be a guidebook for suicides, a few maps to nudge us toward lonely bridges and tempting ledges. Without the tarnish of beer cans and old cellophane, without the mutter of cigarette butts left by those who actually pretended to look at the view instead of analyzing how far and long it would take to jump.

Perhaps I will invent one.

I'LL TELL HIM the truth.

"I wanted to love Trieste and failed. I roamed that city

looking for models or prisoners. Like Sir Richard Burton sitting as British consul in Trieste and remembering his own translations. One thousand and one nights he sat up rewriting that endless tale with its endless telling and all to avoid a death. Scheherazade, you see, did not want to die. I do."

"Shhhh," he'll whisper. "Shhhhhh."

HE'LL MAKE ME forget the unreadable compilation of living, how events and gestures interlock from necessity and habit, every behavior caused by particular sources.

Is there a pattern then? Is it possible to hold life's years up to the light and see a kaleidoscope pattern? Can a physician extract humiliation from a heart and use it as balm to soothe the very heart so injured?

What is the material of a life? Birth leading to death, those mere parentheses?

I will remain a runaway, a hideout, believing that what has hurt me most can cure me. If my life has been choked by would-be assassins, then it will be time for me to choose my own assassin. And he'll do well. I'm not his first.

He'll try to deter me by making me tell him stories about my travels, my itinerant impressions of the world, how, desperate for danger, I roamed the rump neighborhoods of cities, how I was smiled at but left untouched, unmolested, when I longed to be robbed, when I was eager to come upon myself sprawled in the gutter.

Too many potential assassins saw me, eyed me and smiled, but my face warned them away.

THE TASTE OF a madeleine. It was just a cookie.

Shall I confess that the most popular name for a marriage broker is Tomb?

My insatiable restlessness will turn me into a hotel, coming and going personified.

The chinook will blow and wane, the dark arch of the sky will tear away, and the cold brilliant sun will freeze the world again. But I will no longer need to worry or care.

I AM A traveler on my way to bed, to sleep, perchance to dream.

Is DEATH A happy ending?

Acknowledgments

I offer heartfelt gratitude to
  Nicole Markotić, for her incisive editing;
  Brian Stanko, for resilient research;
  Dennis Johnson, for his patience and vision;
  Suzette Mayr, for her suicide dinners;
  Rosemary Nixon, for the suggestion of silence;
  Robert Sharp, for endless support.

I want to thank Fred Wah, Pauline Butling, Pamela McCallum, Yasmin Ladha, Jeanne Perreault, Elizabeth Flagler, Adrienne Kertzer, Maggie Osler, Tamara Pianos, Anna Rutherford, Katja Pfrommer, Leona Gom, and Christl Verduyn, who helped in exactly the right way at the right time, who made me laugh and kept me writing.

Heather Macaulay, Public Relations Manager at the Palliser Hotel, was helpful and informative. The Palliser Hotel does not cater to suicides, fictional or otherwise.

Harry M. Sanders' work on the Palliser Hotel, *The Castle by the Tracks*, provided invaluable historical background.

Especial thanks to Steve Dearden and Yorkshire and Humberside Arts for my time in Yorkshire as International Writer-in-Residence.

Monty Reid's brilliant book, *Dog Sleeps: Irritated Texts,* was a solace and an inspiration, the perfect book to accompany my character.